T0101850

# REVENGE OF THE SCAPEGOAT

Copyright © 2022 by Caren Beilin
Third printing

All rights reserved, including the right of reproduction in whole or in part in any form. This book is a work of fiction. Names, characters, places, and incidents either are products of the author's imagination or are used fictitiously.

This text appropriates lines from the following:
Girard, Rene. Translated by Yvonne Freccero. *The Scapegoat*. pp. 3, 5. © 1986
Johns Hopkins University Press.
Reprinted with permission of Johns Hopkins University Press.

Art on cover by Ernst Ludwig Kirchner
*Female Artist*, 1910
oil on canvas, 101 x 76 cm

The publisher wishes to thank Cora Lewis and Precious Musa.

Library of Congress Cataloging-in-Publication Data
Names: Beilin, Caren, author.
Title: Revenge of the scapegoat / Caren Beilin.
Description: St. Louis, MO: Dorothy, a Publishing Project, [2022]
Identifiers: LCCN 2021038240 (print) | LCCN 2021038241 (ebook) | ISBN
    9781948980074 (paperback; acid-free paper) | ISBN 9781948980081 (ebook)
Subjects: LCGFT: Novels.
Classification: LCC PS3602.E384 R48 2022 (print) | LCC PS3602.E384
    (ebook) | DDC 813/.6—dc23
LC record available at https://lccn.loc.gov/2021038240
LC ebook record available at https://lccn.loc.gov/2021038241

ISBN: 978-1-948980-07-4

Design and composition by Danielle Dutton
Printed on permanent, durable, acid-free recycled paper in the United States of America

Dorothy, a publishing project books are distributed to the trade by New York Review Books
Dorothy, a publishing project | St. Louis, MO

DOROTHYPROJECT.COM

# REVENGE OF THE SCAPEGOAT
## ///
## CAREN BEILIN

DOROTHY, A PUBLISHING PROJECT

# PART I / GOOD KARMA

I was upset.

I was at a café in Philadelphia at a spiking hot metal table in the front. This was last year in early July. I was wearing a marigold jumpsuit, for which bees were favoring me. Or are bees around anyone at any outside table no matter the color you wear?

The wind wasn't vigorous. It is probably grandiose to think that bees surround you in all their limited supply, but I thought that.

I wore red lipstick with purple x's mixed into it kind of thing. And dark-green shoes. I had on very very dark-green shoes, a black-green vegan leather more like a liquid you would press from a hot tampon you are pulling now, by the lamplight, out of a toad's omnibus of Anaïs Nin.

I had been thinking a lot lately about the role I'd played in my family, as their scapegoat. I was thirty-six now, but it still affected me and especially in this week that had brought me a reminder—a package.

People said "Burn it."

Maurice in the adjunct office said, "Iris, burn those letters down. The play, too." He laughed, already looking at some other stuff. Some of his stuff. People who like you so much, like Maurice, don't naturally want to dwell on these sorts of problems with you. You're too good for these problems, and other things, politics, the socius, other books are way more interesting.

And Hilary in Cleveland had said, "You can't keep those in your house with you. Iris."

I could hear her little Bialetti conjuring up a coffee over the phone. A simple yet sophisticated procedure.

I didn't want to burn the letters though. "No, I won't do that, Plum."

Hilary's name, Hilary Plum. I always thought, if someone was falling in love with her, a fruit surname like that would irresist them to her forever.

Plum said, "Oh?"

"If a package like this gets sent to my house, Plum, this evil package, I will be forced to use every last bit of it up"—I meant in my writing. Was this package the right thing for my absolute, eviscerating use? I thought about that myth of the Native person and his buffalo, how in middle school it is said that the Native person uses every last bit of a buffalo, and I would be stripping this package down and using up every last piece of it. The Native person uses, in the schooldays teaching, even the bowels of a buffalo, as a bag for weeds (herbs) or water.

2

It's simple, I had to turn the negative, this dastardly package that arrived out of nowhere for me, hurting me greatly, into a positive. For a big use. When I was done with it, I fantasized, there'd be no package left as there are no bison, no wild bison any longer. This is the wrong metaphor. Maybe the package was more like a bomb than a bison, and I, instead of being in this analogy like a Native person, was more like a thirty-six-year-old white woman but a detective, too, who with my wits was meant to dismantle all this stuff. You can't throw a bomb out in the garbage, or, as Maurice suggested before leaving for his science class designed for artists at the arts college, burn the bomb up. You have to *lean in* to the bomb, more a Cheryl Sandberg type than an Indigenous person. But it was not lost on me at all that we were sitting in the adjunct office on Broad St. on all this Lenape territory, and that these Lenape, contrary to plaques, never signed a treaty, and that we who live do so in a gruesome aridity.

The problem was how to use and/or dismantle it. The package's harm was very specific to me. I was my family's scapegoat. There was hatred I was meant to hold in the place of a loved self. The letters included in the package delivered to me last July were some of the finest proof of that anyone has ever seen. But there was nothing political, nothing topical to it. This was my own personal turmoilous history with my people. Except that I wanted, most of all, for these letters, in that package, to be made public, to become a topic, that the public should really see this, and publishing should be like that, like a tactic. A book should be like a lot of spit. But who would publish me? Who publishes a person who's sort of soaking in pain, who can't always walk, employed only pretty much in name?

Did writing exist in books anyway these days? I thought, perhaps very defensively. Maybe it didn't.

Where does writing foment? Where does effulgence slip in the innerlining of which writing? That is what I meant.

Maybe writing these days, I thought, was more in the grocery lists, lately such a bunch of just *wish lists*, or at least with the arts students I adjuncted at, real writing flowed out of them when they wrote to me directly to a) accuse me of something and b) let me know why they could not do an assignment or any of the assignments or be anywhere or get to a reading. Why-I-can't or, even better, Why-I-won't writing was better, much much better, than any other writing I was currently reading. It was lively. It seemed to describe the contemporary. But I hardly read.

But students aren't only archival pieces of detriment for an almost gen-x-er like myself to pick through. I think they knew what their literary power was when they wrote me these sometimes problematic emails, considering I was this part-time woman they were dumping all of this No energy onto as if I were their signal oppressor. Maybe in the superlative arc of the universe I was their most approachable oppressor, that's fair, but the best writing for anyone is an accident or at least it feels like a big oblong coincidence. Maybe it does really need to be in the form of a letter. The letters in my package were an evil archive, for sure, a father who hates his own daughter???—no, who wouldn't mind destroying her—no, who desperately needs her love and wants to choke it out of her—who thinks she could sustain these horrible letters. Worst package of my life.

Oh well.

So I'd rather eat this package, I told myself, and use it all up, wear it and beat people with it, than burn it for some kind of psychotherapeutic tirade. Rather smash my face in it than rip its messages like a burnt bandaid off of this earth, tearing trees and daffodils out in the process. Save the daffs. Hey, save daffs. I wanted to perversely walk around with my package, my prize, like a kid who's got some sodden snake out of a pig pit and determines to make out with it. I'd marry this package, if I weren't already. Yuck. I was.

I had been married for five years.

Joe was a recovering alcoholic. He told me that microdosing heroin was helping him in his recovery, from alcohol, so I had been watching him do that on the couch and sitting dinnerside in the kitchen for months inside of this illusion that I was the one who was allowing it, allower, and marriage manager, and like some kind of inspector at the border of his biochemical pastures who could approve (or not) of these different things, such as heroins, and I was the one—I told myself a lot—letting heroins and methamphetamine in in small enough, in reasonable doses, passing through my controls into him, in my fucked up thinking, since it was helping him, I reasoned, with his drinking problem, and people, he told me, are actually doing this.

"They shoot up at the meetings," he said.

He told me he went to meetings.

He told me his microheroins dealer was actually his sponsor.

He said he hadn't drunk anything in years.

At the time of the beginning of this (me sitting at Good Karma, upset), Joe was missing. He'd been missing since earlier. After another argument about a blowjob. I don't think he even wanted one. I think an addict wants to argue, so that they get to leave. Leaving is the first step to using, if you've used everything at home, and he'd torn through all cigarettes, drinks, and heroin like the house was his big wild bison in this problem of a comparison, glugging at the rubbing alcohol—alcoholism is cartoonish and garish and often passes out on its own nose, and getting married is like that, too, like entering into some kind of waking cartoon.

He said he hated me, I was a bitch, because I wouldn't blow him. He probably went to Kensington, northerly neighborhood, with its muddy banks of homelessness and use, and its rolling mountains of charred sleeping bags in reds and oranges and greens like some kind of Montagne Sainte-Victoire of Paul Cézanne's will, and I sat at Good Karma, having finished up my class on writing fiction, waiting for Ray Levy. The package, which sat with me like my little horrid poodle, a slim white USPS box, almost an envelope but not, so that it took on the shape of a hollowed book, contained four things:

1. A typed letter my dad had handed me, in my bedroom, when I was fourteen years old.
2. A typed letter he'd handed to me when I was sixteen years old.
3. A legal pad on which, when I was seventeen years old and leaving soon for college, I had written half of a play I'd titled "Billy the Id."
4.

My dad had sent these things to me again that July, saying in a note that he was clearing out drawers at the old family home in the suburbs, and he'd found these things I must have, as a teenager, taken care to place somewhere. Maybe I'd hid them. I hadn't been back over. It was unclear if he knew what he'd sent. Maybe he didn't know. He'd sent out to me some pile that seemed to be mine. Maybe he hadn't really read through these things. But here they were, things that had torn through me as a teenager sent as a totally perverse encore, at thirty-six, to do their work on me again, like an insane boomerang the stars had drilled strings in.

Everything comes around, but I couldn't believe I'd have to bear these letters twice in one life, and the play? "Billy the Id"? Oh my god! I couldn't believe I wrote that! Who was I? You could say I had pep. I'd wanted to be a playwright. Reading it over again, shocked by what I'd written (its badness, its strange promise), it seemed I must have been reading Edward Albee and Allen Ginsburg and *Naked Lunch* and whatever other males available at the high school library where I remember I also read everything by Lawrence Ferlinghetti, by John Updike, by Anthony Burgess, and ok, Anne Sexton. So embarrassing though, "Billy the Id," good thing I'd never finished it. It seemed, from one of the opening quips of the rapscallion Billy—a character I'd intended as the living embodiment of the id—I believed that John Updike was one of the great beat poets?

Why would I have thought that?

Did I think anyone is a beat poet if they use women as a metaphor? Is a beat poet anyone who exalts and so silos women? Is a beat poet someone who uses his journey as the template for human time? Is a beat poet someone who has a lot of "pubic" episodes? I'd wanted badly to be a beat poet, I remember that. I wanted to be like the great beat poet John Updike. Beat poets like that are like islands, you want to be them, you can't quite see yourself as the drowning type. I envied, admired, and emulated beat poets and I hated my dad so, so much, and thought about killing him, but his letters to me, I mean look at them, I mean, he was the greatest beat poet by these standards, even much better than Updike.

But what I'd really wanted to know, sitting there at Good Karma waiting for Ray, was how did my dad even find my latest address?

I hadn't talked to him in over a decade. My remaining family member—Kenneth, my slightly older brother—knew I wanted nothing to do with him anymore. He'd been begging me to come back into the fold of the family for years, saying stuff like "Things change" and "Dad's mellowed" and "You can't be angry forever," and what did I do? I wore these harsh yellow outfits all the time, this linen stuff, dyed with this kind of dye you can only find or anyway I'd only found it in Tucson, sort of the molten marigold soufflé spilling out boldly onto Tilda Swinton's complete oeuvre of Irigaray? Have you seen this stuff? Why did I always wear such a burning color as marigold? I once felt like I was being burned alive by my dad, when I was a young teenager. You should see these letters. Now I was always wearing the pelt, the harsh linen pelts of how I fucking felt. You leave because shelter is insufficient. Shelter doesn't have all kinds of stuff. I'd been dressing like that for a while.

It was important not to have any contact with my dad, if I were going to move on in my life. I wasn't angry, I was very protective. I couldn't go over the edge of anxiety and panic and depression and feelings of self-abnegation. The letters were already retrograding me hard. I'd barely even looked at my students that day, in our summer class. I'd looked at them like a guilty dog. I walked around like someone was going to kill me if I looked anyone at all in the eye.

But as I waited for Ray at Good Karma, I couldn't stop myself from thinking, Who gave my dad my address?

No, I didn't think anything of that sort. Knowing it was Kenneth . . .

It was Kenneth, I knew.

A scapegoat escapes. You can learn a lot by looking at words. Not using etymology, something the theorist Maurice Blanchot warns us about in grave and clear terms, *thank god*: "Likewise, the radicalization whereby etymology's linkages appear to promise us the security of a native habitat is the hiding place of the homelessness which the ultimate's demand (the eschatological imperative: without finality and without logos) incites in us as uprooted creatures, deprived by language itself of language—of language understood as *ground* where the germinal root would plunge, and as the promise of a developing life." Uprooted creatures, we cannot all be traced back to a source or be understood from the viewpoint of our origin.

Kenneth thought my name was tied to a tree at our dad's house, basically. He would go over there, to the suburbs, and call me from there, and say I should come over and be part of this dinner. Everyone was over, he said. My nieces. Old cousins. Our dad's girlfriend. I do not want to study the etymological root of anything but it's obvious to me from looking at "scapegoat" that it describes that it escaped. It left. There were two goats. They were siblings. One stayed and one now lives in the desert outside the walls of the village. Kenneth sent—I couldn't forget—cell phone images of my people in the back-yard, eating barbecue, sitting around on a deck I used to lie down on, sometimes naked when I cut school and used mushrooms, using the deck as a launchpad into any number of wormholes. The air had such a texture of these holes. I knew it then. But then I became older and weaker. I was with Brandon and Lisa in Tucson when Kenneth's pics came onto my phone and I bawled.

"Why don't you come over, too?" he texted. "We want you here."

I'm in Tucson visiting Lisa and Brandon, I thought, and also—you all ran me out. I can't ever return.

The village lives because the scapegoat is outside of its walls. That's obviously what a scapegoat does for everyone. I liked my life. The desert, on my most recent visit, made my joints, which I'd found out so recently were eroding from this autoimmune disease, feel quite good. When I finally got around to the visit, in May, to see Lisa and Brandon, my autoimmune arthritis receded—amazing—into ig-noble seeds tucked sparingly up the calcified sleeves of some stray bones. It became almost like nothing. There was an outdoor shower on their rented land. You could watch a hawk fly over your shower. Jesus fucking christ. If you have a friend with an outdoor shower, you've escaped something, if you have these friends.

Out walking in the desert in the morning, Lisa told me creosote on the ground communicates, via compiling all its resins, with the clouds, promoting rain whenever it wants some water. The resin is like a phone. The desert is really good. Anti-anxiety. A scapegoat loves that. When I was first out there, at eighteen, after I'd left my dad's house basically on fire, going to school and finding such a one as Lisa to live with, that's when my dad did it, slaughtered up Kenneth.

That is what happens to the other goat. You can read about it in the Bible or on Wikipedia. And then I eventually did move back to Philadelphia.

And now that Kenneth was killed but living and procreating he was causing even more problems, giving out my address like this, so I called him up.

Upset. Mad.

"Did you tell Dad where I live?"

A bee was flying in and out of my jumpsuit.

It's not going to sting me, is what I was thinking. Because it doesn't want to die. A hive is not around. A bee doesn't develop a personal vendetta. Even if I upset it quite a lot. A bee is only a terrorist. It would never kill itself without a politics backing it up, and the hive is political and there's no hive in any of these trees near here. I've looked up. I've checked it out. And I feel more comfortable around bees, around women, and all kinds of terrorism than around many many many men. Men are terrorists, fine, they are, but men are authors, too, lots of those, but not all men are writers. You don't want to be with a man in a house. I'd rather be in a school than a house in terms of abuse. I'd rather be killed outside, on a stage, than beaten indoors for more than five years.

Ray came right on time, at 7 p.m. I really thought they might be late. That's why I called Kenneth, mad, to pass time, like one of those bookless people you see, but now they were already here. So they sat down as I continued on with my call.

"Just throw it out. If you don't like what's in the package he sent, throw it away, Iris."

"But, Kenneth—Kenneth—it should never have been sent. He shouldn't know where I live."

"Dad was clearing out some drawers. Finis."

"But Kenneth, I do not feel safe. I do not want him to know where I am these days."

We could not even agree on the premise. Plus I'd been living in this house that had been our mom's, her secret. It was supposed to be her escape house. But she'd never moved there. She rented it out for years, a secret landlord from the suburbs. She'd bought it when I was eight, Kenneth ten, when we could have all left together intact. But she got really sick.

In the biblical story, in this wikibiblical tale, they kill the goat that's kept around, and who doesn't even have a name. Othergoat? Does it even have a name or any hobbies? My dad didn't even pay attention to Kenneth while he killed him up. He was still talking about me, how bad I was, what a rotten person, blaming me and really fascinated by me, obsessed with whether or not I was a lesbian, and thinking about where I would have gone (Tucson, first) while he sort of dully, kind of bored, definitely bookless, passed the knife through Kenneth, over the phone or at a bbq, ignoring everything about him.

"Dad's harmless. He's out of it, Iris."

When you are the scapegoat in your family, your body becomes your family. When you get sick, your body begins talking to you, too.

The letters my father handed me when I was fourteen and sixteen had made me want to murder myself. I remember sitting in my bedroom, holding one of the letters, whichever one, whatever, and being embarrassed. The letter, in one year and then the other one, stabbed me. To be this despised, it's so embarrassing. The letter was like a corner; a suicide is despairing but it's despair picked up by prowling pragmatism. I thought I might need to kill myself like Anne Sexton, and I was looking at a peach tree (the window) desperate, the bees crusting the peaches in their behavior. I wanted to die taking in the size of the statements in the letter. There were his eyeballs being pumped in, hating everything they saw. The dastardly eyeballs were burning me up, the eyeballs were spinning and I was overdosing on them, too much of it coming into me or just too quick. The letter, whichever one, each in their year, made my fingers turn white, the blood leapt away from that computer paper—that he'd *typed* it—my fingers didn't want to have anything to do with it. My fingers had teen ibex blood in them. My fingers were really awesome. If I'd had the wherewithal in that suicidal moment to look into a mirror, I might have noticed that my eyes were becoming very thick wanting to block the letter from entering. There were boards being nailed up over my pupils, but language is less like a hurricane you can prepare for in that way and more like a perfume or toxin spreading with infusing sensations, mindlessly. The letter was touching my brain and I was crying.

I thought of all the bushes on the street, the secret parlors and ballrooms of the squirrels, the fantasy of living in trees in the anterooms of the owls, of going to live with an uncle, but the uncles were off. They were upset on their own gnarled paths. A triplicate of dead aunts.

Kenneth said on the phone, "Dad was clearing out your old bedroom drawers. He wanted to return your things to you. It was all innocent."

"This package, Kenneth, has some consequence to my emotions. I did not know these letters still existed nor did I plan on ever seeing them again."

"Just throw it out. If you don't like what's in there, just, Iris, throw it all away."

"But it should never have been sent!" I was losing it.

"I doubt he even knew what he was sending. He's old. He was just cleaning up."

"But do you think a woman should receive these letters twice, in one lifetime? Now, in her thirty-sixth year? Is that fair?"

*Just* is a word Kenneth would use quite a lot, as I would use *quite*, so much, and it made any sentence, this *just*, into whining, no pleading, no worse, it's pleasing. It is the worst word. More used by women who can't get a grip in a conversation for reasons of gender oppression but Kenneth felt like that victim, too, somewhere in there. After all, he was killed. My dad killed him while I ran on fire in my jumpsuit bucking and escaping. It expresses modesty—*I just want*—while giving permission—*just do it*—and contributes to temporonormativity—*I just made it!*—as if no one would wait for you, and *just* is used to express a confounded disappointment, as in *I just wish you would have, I just wanted you to*, it expresses the capacity of the speaker for whom things are *just*, easy, are fine, as if nothing happened to anyone, as if Kenneth hadn't beaten me with my mother's cane, at my father's request, when my mother couldn't walk, when she watched, *just throw it out*, or *just stop already*, the *just* is a thrust of violent exasperation, as if people can stop, while also connoting invitation, warmth, *hey, just ask*, the word could sauce, can soil and pitch its bullshit in any sentence, is used notoriously by women who plead, who can't help but plead, who say it, *just*, because they are begging you, born into a pitiful life of hoping, *just*, just help me, and *I hope that you, I hoped that you would, I'd just hoped for help*, that word, my mother's word, hope or help, each as sick as she. I tried eradicating *just* from my entire vocabulary. At least over emails. At least over professional emails. I tried to hold myself forcibly back from saying it, from begging and hoping, from needing any help from anyone, whereas *quite* holds you up, *quite* hoists, but Kenneth, killèd Kenneth, heavily sauced all his sentences with *just*. But a scapegoat—that's me!—is addicted to justice. Even though justice is damned, is wed to return.

The grown scapegoat takes joy out of many minor things, is an inveterate nature lover and walker, synesthesia and wonder have been sparked, after you've developed your own self in a horrible bedroom, in that fetid twilight marinade refusing suicide barking at peaches in a pact with the unrevealed.

And here I was in my reveries keeping Ray waiting. But Ray was so, so stepped on in this life, they didn't even mind. They sat there still, so stilly, like a dik-dik confronting a road sign.

I took this time to reflect.

The petite rowhome on Naudain St. (my mother's place) was moldy and had many shadows. The sun came through two inadequate front windows giving off only some perishing squares on the teak floor. I liked to stand in a square of light right as it hit at its most wholesome, at 11 a.m., gone by 11:15. The house was not so hot. Asbestos in there, the walls were infected and the bathroom was broken, it was a mildew estuary and its statuary—tub, sink—overrun with molds from orange to green to black and wet. Perhaps this was a matter of cleaning up but the house was being eaten by subvegetation and shadows bred with each other right on the counter, a gray loam fisting and kissing a gray blob. It was a difficult house. My mom never lived in it with us, though she'd planned to. She'd have taken us with her. Right around that time, that time when my dad started repeating things about my being the devil. Around the time Kenneth started using her cane like a baseball bat, my dad like a mob boss, and me flickering and bleeding into a goat shape. But she got way too sick. She needed a whole wheelchair. She needed to empty her bowels in bed. There was a sickness volcano in her genetics, in the MS, and like the famous Vesuvius where you can see what things were like, old lovers and other selves were petrified inside of her arms and legs, which couldn't move any longer. Her life froze. And she died in bed.

Marrièd.

She died when I was nineteen. She died of staying.

Kenneth called me in Tucson, to say as much, but I didn't come back just then.

I should not have married Joe. Old high school boyfriend, I saw him when I moved back, at the point where I really needed my mother's house. No job. I was drowning while many men were sunning on their islands. I saw him outside of it. He was walking down Naudain, like he'd dropped something and was looking around, he must have been looking for viable cigarettes or, really, needles. I'd kicked out the renters, art students, and then found them again in my classes at the arts college, displaced and rightfully wary of me. I was an adjunct. I had no investment in them. I taught a class on menstruation in fiction and it filled right up. Everyone wanted to talk about their period. Everybody's period was really bad. But did they want to write? I married. We tried to sell my mother's house and go live in Tucson. I told Joe about the creosote and about Lisa and Brandon, maybe we'd become similar to them. Good to one another. Interested. Tidy. But we couldn't sell the house at all. We showed it to people who didn't want it. I cleaned it up. Other couples, it always was a couple, on Saturday mornings, like we were making a swinger's date, and I brewed tea. I boiled cinnamon in a pot overnight to change the house's vibe. And I'd told Kenneth firmly, "I'm back in Philly but do not tell Dad." I was inside the village walls. City of blame. The cashiers everywhere looked at me like they were going to write me a letter. They rung me up like they were typing something.

Ray said they were going into Good Karma to order some coffee and would return to our little front table.

Kenneth hung up on me. His children had been roiling around him. His wife, he'd said, was on a walk.

I waited for Ray. My feet hurt. I could barely walk. You couldn't take them anywhere. All I could manage was to class, the adjunct office, and home again. Once I sat by the fountain in Rittenhouse, mid-way home, willing myself. Someone came up to me who always comes up to people, who always asks if he can talk to me. He has on his face some kind of marketing smirk. Marketing is coming, but I have no idea what he is selling. He looks interested in me but there's a sneer to his interest, it's hurtful. I hate when he approaches. What does he want? I can't ever find out because I always need to say, "No." He even persists, "Can't I ask you one little question?" I hate how he treats me, handling me cutely. He says surely I don't want to be alone. I don't want to kick him. I'm having a hard time taking a step. I'm aware that I look radiant, young, and lithe in my jumpsuit, like a superhero urbanite. But I cannot step. Should I ask him a question, for help? What could he do? I didn't know what my feet needed. The bone of them was coming open.

I would only say to him, "Please go away, I'm not interested. All I want is to sit here alone."

He didn't have any pamphlets. What was he selling? What did he want? I knew I was being addressed as a dupe of some kind but what kind? Sexual? Romantic? As someone who would probably sign up for a magazine subscription? I felt he could see, from his vantage, what seemed doable, usable, risible, I don't know. I doubt I seemed like anything at all, that was my problem. He was talking to me from somewhere where I wasn't, like the wrong reader picking up de Beauvoir in a used bookstore only because a book like *The Mandarins*, at 608 pages, is thick enough to use to stop doors, and that's why this person was in this store, to find something to use because he'd been wanting to keep his door open, and I hated not being really read. I hate that. Not even the title.

Not that I'm de Beauvoir but still.

"My feet hurt," I told him. "Please go away."

He smiled a smile that was obviously not his smile. He looked as desperate as someone who is being sex trafficked, but predatorial.

"Those pretty feet?" sort of thing is what he said . . .

I thought of calling Joe, not because of this but for the feet, but what would he do? Would he carry me blocks home? Could he bring shoes that were more cushioned or maybe rollerskates I could glide in? I put my feet into the fountain, as I used to do all the time in this same spot when I was a teenager, before they ever chlorinated it, when it was a dark enchanting green, not this fake blue, like pornstar water, I thought, the way pornstars even out all their colors so nothing is murky or dark or real and the genital area is completely paratactic with the breast, the ass, the face, as this fake blue was now acting paratactically and pornographically with the blue bright sky, a polo shirt, the frosted undertuft of a bird. The fountain water was cool and refreshing. I sat for as long as I needed. The man had gone away from me but sat close by and looked at me. This always happened.

Why didn't he ever go ahead and simply ask me the question?

He must not have remembered me. He must have asked this question about if he could ask a question to so many people every day, and this is why I said no. There wasn't a question, how could there be? If there was a question he would ask it. I don't know what it would be but it would be something worse than a question. Nobody is that nice, to check and see if you will allow yourself to be asked a question. He was asking, I was sure, if he could do something much worse. Most people are so mean. But this must have been really mean, what he wanted to say or do. He wanted a "Yes" to the wrong thing, yes-you-can-ask-me-your-question, but he would take it and use this "Yes" and do something absolutely unspeakable with it, I had no idea what. I could not imagine.

"It's just one little question," he would say. The *just* tipped me off. And the "little," the way he spoke to me like I was a cute and stunned kid on a TV show and he was the host, helping me through these entertaining obstacles. I wonder if he was doing some kind of God's work, but he looked too suave for that. And too empty-handed.

"I would leave," I told him, "but my feet are killing me so please go away from me."

"Are you sure?"

"Yes."

I could see my feet in the fountain's water, what I never saw as a teenager. You used to put them in there and they'd go somewhere. In this newly chlorinated clarity they did look inordinately swollen, but only to my eye, which had watched them for so long. They were like my children, the way I'd watched them all their life, but grown up, doing their own thing now. It was painful. They looked like two old retired men.

I named them Bouvard and Pécuchet. I guess I was thinking of that Flaubert novel, the one only lit majors and bookstore owners read, *Bouvard and Pécuchet*. Published 1881, one year after he died. They are old men who retire together. A bit early for retirement but Bouvard has unexpected money, a surprise inheritance. Someone who dies is surprisingly his dad. Bouvard and Pécuchet haven't known each other all of life, though. They meet, at the last moment, in Paris, and Pécuchet takes note, they have both written their names on the inside of their caps. They fall in love I think. They leave for the country, together. They'll start a new life. They are fools, and the novel is a lapidary circle.

I looked at them, these total fools, floating in the fountain, but they were friends. In the book, Pécuchet exclaims, right off the bat, "How good it would be to be in the country!" right when they meet, starting things. I put them closer to each other in the water. I touched one to the other and the other touched him. Bouvard started in the right foot, he said, "The students, you know, are not right in the head."

Bouvard mused, "Their eyes will scrape the end of the world, I think. Good for them. *Last witness, end of history, close of a period, turning point, crisis.*" He was whispering viciously some Blanchot line I'd read recently—

Pécuchet, on the left, countered, "We'll all be gone in the cigarettes by then, right Bouvard? There will never be no smokers. Smoking is one of the least harmful things. Think of *things*."

"What *things*, Pécuchet, must I think of now? What? Smoking might not be as harmful as a nuclear holocaust on its surface but it could be *sinister*, and it could be a *synecdoche*. It might make our lungs into hives of a kind of anti-honey. The human lung, I'm sure, is the split empire of The End. Cigarettes are surely awful."

"Bouvard. *You* smoke."

"C'est une pipe!"

At Good Karma each retiree—my two feet—was cloaked in a very dark-green vegan leather shoe, impatient as ever. Of course they dreamed of the country. They wanted to get out. They despised

Philly, walking near or atop many steaming grates. So much bypassing of streams of people's piss. They felt so stiff. I could walk so much less than a mile. A block and a half? My shoes were all bed convertibles at this point. My joints were separating and eroding and I'd soon need a cane. I would try to look unlike that, though. I'd cross my legs, to be jaunty. Bouvard hated to dangle down like this, over atop Pécuchet. He'd scream "Put me down!" and I wouldn't.

I tried to tell my students such things, like, you can't simply make up a character. Pain springs them, bonkers, out of the walls and out of body parts. If anyone ever stabs me in my cunt, I'm sure Jane Eyre herself will show her glorious face.

In pain all year, I'd been diagnosed six months earlier with the rheumatoid arthritis. Waiting still for Ray (they must have ordered some elaborate latte . . . ) a bee now stooped into my coffee. Zoomed right down and drilled into it, maybe it was an idiot. Or it sensed there was honey in the bottom of my cup. Smart. I had no choice but to throw my coffee quickly into the air. Bees are in trouble.

Ray caught it.

Now they were soaked in coffee, and honey, and you could see right through their white short-sleeved buttondown. Ray wasn't burned, I hoped, because of their binder, which remained obscure. They didn't even mention what had happened, typical. We'd been friends for a long time.

"Hey. What the hell happened to your shoulder?"

My shoulder had a purple mark.

Joe had complained, before sleep, that I did not offer to blow him. I had not blown him at all lately. He attempted to show me something about blowing him using his finger, the way P.E. teachers coat the condom deeply down some bananas, those perilously rotting cock manikins.

Joe was sucking off his own finger showing me how he'd want me to do it to his cock. He wanted to blow himself, I thought, look, he had ideas, the way he sucked with a technique. The way I wanted students to write. He looked so good at it, sucking off his own finger, treating it as a cock synecdoche, showing off what he'd do to himself if he were myself and I were someone who blows someone when they said they don't drink but are so, so drunk.

I told him, "I do blow, but I don't a flaccid person. This is a limit that I have."

"It will grow hard in your mouth."

"You'll fall asleep."

We argued.

"Not if you do it exactly this way."

God, what was I doing to my students?

He wanted me to follow this technique. He wanted this prefab blowjob cut from the blowprints in his own mouth so inbred with vodka.

A blowjob doesn't work like that. Technique isn't desire.

"I'm going to sleep. I can't believe you've been smoking in our bed," I said.

He burned me on my shoulder, in the middle of the night.

"I can't sleep," Joe said. And, "I'm going out."

A few days had passed, and now, at Good Karma, it was a waxy violet hole. I hadn't even felt it burning up my skin when it was waking me up. I simply was waking and I felt really worried. I'd said, "Where are you going to go right now?"

Bouvard and Pécuchet had been roused that night as well. Bouvard had had a splitting headache that pounded in all of my right toes. Pécuchet seemed to be fucking his own asshole with a knife, but it was weird. If I looked down at my foot it looked serene, like nothing, not like a person, first of all, or an old French man or whatever, but also like nothing at all was even happening. As though I were not in extreme pain. It looked the way it looks when you look at the moon. You can't feel the moon when you look at it. You can't even really imagine it. You can't even think about what's happening inside of it, you think it's really inside of you, magnetically, mythically, literarily. I looked at my feet that looked like nothing, like a wedge of meat-light in the sheets in the moonlight, looking nothing at all how they felt, so horrible.

"I can't sleep!" Joe put things in a bag. He was going to go. I saw him packing up the tools he used to microdose heroin all of the time.

"Where are you going to go?"

I guess I really needed to get married, like a bridge to someplace else. A fortress around me there in Philly. I believed in the strike of coincidence. Why was he on Naudain St. at night, at my house unwittingly, the very night I arrived? I thought that was amazing, and in high school he had helped me deal with my family by fucking me in a beautiful park, but it did not occur to me that Philadelphia is just, tiny. It is quite small. I had never lived there, in Center City, as an adult. But I'd soon learn: you see people you used to know on its little streets at the strangest of times all of the time. He wasn't looking for me. Life wasn't showing me *him*. He was just there, looking for needles.

Romance, to a scapegoat, is like some kind of proof. They all could not be right, they who were wrong about me. To scapegoat is to wrong someone so young.

I didn't know what to tell Ray about it. I didn't want to be boring.

"Joe . . ." Was joking? Was kidding around? It was art?

"Oh."

"I like that little bandana."

"Thanks."

"That bandana . . ."

"Shut up, Iris. You're patronizing me. All my clothes are shit. This is, like, this is a shit short-sleeve wrinkle-free buttondown that I got off of Amazon seven years ago."

28

"A no-wrinkle Amazon . . ."

"Yeah."

"It doesn't look wrinkled."

"It does not wrinkle."

Ray continued, "My entire memory of being young is a wave of pain that never ends. Like, social pain. I think I'm more functional now and clearly I can get over it in certain instances, but I mean it was the biggest disservice my parents did, never addressing it, because it was also indicative of so much more going on. I was even held back for it. I think there were certain milestones one had to hit to begin first grade or something but one of them was, like, *talking*. And I didn't. I wouldn't even talk to go to the bathroom, I'd just piss myself. I couldn't ask. So embarrassing."

"I couldn't ask as well. I pissed myself as well."

"Really?"

"But also, the people at my nursery school were sometimes not that nice about the bathroom, I remember. It was a little intimidating to ask them. They were, like, tired."

"All of my memories are of being a small kid crammed into a small bathroom with the other kids and the teachers are changing all of us because I'd pissed and leaked onto them because we were all sitting on the floor."

"In this case it really was your fault."

We'd been talking in this series of cafés about our experiences being the scapegoat of our families. I was taping and transcribing these for a book no one would publish and I told Ray, who was down, that I'd use their exact language. We talked about it.

"I say keep the name Ray," they'd said. "I think I would feel more tender toward the character if he shared my name."

We knew Ray would arc towards *he* by the end of the book, maybe the real Ray with him.

I told them at Good Karma, "One of my bad early memories of being in preschool is that I pissed myself in the gym and you have to, you know, go report yourself. So I went up and was like, 'I peed,' so then I had to go to this other area and report that I'd peed to some of the other preschool teachers who were having their lunch."

"Oh my god, I wouldn't be able to say it."

"It was all horrifying. And then they were eating lunch and so they said, 'Ok, you need a new pair of underwear,' and they were like, 'You're going to have to find a pair in the lost-and-found bin.'"

"Gross."

"And so there was this trunk in the hallway, my preschool was in the basement of a church, and they were like, 'Go in that hallway, you have to be in this hallway with this trunk, looking through it.'"

"It sounds like a fairy tale. Like Rumpelstiltskin. You have to spin this straw into gold."

"This trunk was really enormous. Endless clothes. But there was no underwear in the trunk. Nobody lost their underwear. I'd go back and tell them. I'd say, 'There isn't any.' And they'd say, 'Look again.'"

"It really is like a fairy tale. And then on the third time you find a maxi pad, which isn't underwear but—will work, you know."

"I guess I could put it in my dirty underwear. But wouldn't that maxi pad be used? I mean, you wouldn't want this stuff."

"Not necessarily. It could be in its wrapper. Not everything lost would be used. Now if it were a fairy tale what you'd find is some *magical underwear*, some magical britches, and that would be the start of the plot that unfolds from there. You would then get your revenge on those teachers eating lunch. All of their sandwiches would turn soggy with pee, because that's what the britches do. They move your pee to some other object. And then one of them has this horrifying thought, which you would never know cause fairy tales don't have interiority, but she develops a taste for it but she represses it immediately."

We thought about that.

Ray said, "My surgery is this week."

Ray worked as a copywriter for a medical devices firm that anchored itself across from a complex of hospitals. They wrote to the hospitals to educate them about the devices that were being manufactured in Quakertown, PA, and to promote types of surgery for problems typically cured by time, herbs, coconut oil, and maybe a little Prednisone.

Ray wrote letters of inquiry (devious marketing actually) to

31

mostly gynecologists. They mugged as some kind of expert, but that's writing. That's copywriting. Grammar, I'd told plenty of students, is marketing. Ray's boss was the owner of a closed autoparts factory. He hired consultants to find uses for his heaps of materials that were sitting around. The devices Ray promoted with writing were amalgams of many kinds of car metals, coated in rubbers made from actual car tires, and these remixed cars miniaturized and implanted, sometimes stapled or nailed into people with urethras, vaginas, or wombs, seemed to be causing a few autoimmune-like issues. Problems near to death, but not death. Death is a line. It was Ray's job, too, to overwrite these issues to the doctors.

To ride over the pain.

It did pain them. They'd said about it earlier, at a different café, I think we were at the Ultimo on Catherine St., "I'm in this bad profession, but what else is there to do in Philly besides work in the medical industry or at Penn. But you have to have gone there to, like, check people in at the museum there or whatever. And I can't afford to adjunct like you. I have loans. It's a privilege to be a good person. Or even to seem like one."

They continued at Good Karma, "So I get to choose if I want my nipples back on or not."

They smiled grimly and handsomely. Ray was very dashing, with an aquiline nose like a nose in a sketch.

They continued, "I can't decide. Some people get tattoos of nipples instead."

"Maybe I'd get that. Like this. Two purple holes."

"Enter the purple voids."

"My nipples are so erect. It would be nice if they were flat like tattoos for once."

"I love how you are. It's obscene. Look at you in that jumpsuit."

"I don't love how you look. You'll be much better off without breasts. It's not you at all, how you are. I feel impatient about this. I'm glad it's coming up so soon."

"Well, come on—"

Ray, blushing, looking fluffed up and cool, to be complimented.

Ray knew I was in need of continuing our conversations. Bouvard and Pécuchet were really listless at this point. They were impatient to go, but I don't think they believed I'd really do it. Pull the trigger and leave Philly forever? Bouvard had some kind of big inheritance he wanted to use to get out of Paris and start up a life with Pécuchet in the country, fine. But a scapegoat doesn't do the inheriting. What did I have? Let's be clear. I had a little over four grand from my miserly ways. And the house, which I don't think my mother left to me so much as hid with my name.

It's inefficient, if they had to kill the other goat anyway. The Kenneth. Isn't all their sin supposed to leave with the scapegoat, when she goes running off? Isn't that the point? But they kill Othergoat anyway. They're nuts.

A scapegoat is very gentle, re-parented by the crucial cosmos, if poorly. The stars do not have any language or money. But I had that house. My mother did leave it to me, like a moldy letter, black blotches all over, and all over the counters.

I continued at Good Karma, "You're the only friend I know who was also the family scapegoat. It's not like other people didn't live with viciousness. But the narrative was so well defined in my house. I was to blame. What about you?"

"My gloss on it is that—I mean, I had two parents and two siblings and nobody had real feelings for one another and, um, the children were raised without real feelings, so we were even I think more compromised than our parents, like there was so much emotional dysfunction and probably genuine antagonistic feelings, and my mother is also some kind of sociopath probably so she was also kind of overtly aggressing against people and making things worse. There was no way for—We weren't religious. There was nothing bringing us together."

I had told Ray earlier, "My dad was this lapsed Orthodox . . ."

They said at Good Karma, "I happened to be a kind of outwardly—I outwardly am negative. That's just my affect. So I think the only way the family could maintain any sense of coherence was

through a scapegoating mechanism. To blame all of the negative affects on the ones I was outwardly expressing and showing, and then
they'd maintain some kind of unity."

I had told them, "He told them, he said it explicitly to my
mother and brother, 'It's her, it's Iris, she's ruining things,' and
he told Kenneth to take my mother's cane, to go beat me with it.
Right at the table. I don't know if they all applauded but I think
they watched. They nodded or zoned out or something. In a fog
of terrified approval. It was like a ritual, a trance. And whenever
he left, my dad, storming clothes into a bag and getting ready to
initiate Abandon, it was said: I am leaving because of Iris. And
then Kenneth, my brother, shook me like shaking me down and
begging, 'Just make him stay, we don't know how to give Mom
her medicine. Just tell him to stay here.' The scapegoat is so weird.
Hated but like, so revered, I'm this wizard. Ten years old, but I'm
like packed with power. Kenneth would have been twelve. It was
true. Could we have handled any needles? We couldn't inject anything into our mom at that time, how young is that, and she really
couldn't move."

Ray's thought on that one was: "The scapegoat's *a renewing*. It's
kind of this strange renewing force in the family. It allows the others
to unite. So I don't know, that's what I think was happening with me.
But I wasn't a very happy child and I was always kind of expressing
negative views and emotions, and they would get quite upset with

me. I, like, ruined vacations, I ruined anything, anything you can imagine, just even a trip to get ice cream I would ruin, so—"

The sun was beginning to set outside of Good Karma. An early summer sunset, after 8 p.m.

Ray continued, "Like once even, I'm already getting messed up in my head thinking I ruined this but I didn't, it was an accident, but like once we were driving to Boston for my cousin's bat mitzvah. We were late of course because my family's really dysfunctional and can't do anything, but that morning I woke up and my earring was caught inside my ear. It had migrated inside my ear in this really disturbing way and no one could get it out. We were already late but we had to stop at the emergency room and get it cut out of my ear and we missed the bat mitzvah. We got there that night after it was over. So then my entire extended family blamed me. For ruining the bat mitzvah."

The sun was a burning cloche roasting something green. It had multiple crystal pits. The scapegoat needs the sun, and the moon. Throwing a rocking chair at my head, a cabbage, telling me what I did to him, to make him do this to me, and to the family. He was going to leave my sick mom in her bed, full of piss and lumps of shit, because of me.

Ray continued, "They would say something like, 'Of course you all are always late.' They'd say, 'I can't believe you missed this, but it's not unexpected that you missed this.' And then it would be like,

'Well, it's Ray.' So I would be kind of like, the blame, yeah, the source of the blame, the target."

I told them, "Fried with abuse, with threats, with being chased, I remember being so solemn around my grandparents. 'What's wrong with her,' my grandmother would ask. 'She gets like this,' this was my mother's talking. It was coming from in me, this venom. My bad nature. My brother shrieking in the backseat as my dad threatened me in the front, speeding down the highway, 'Make him stop, stop this, Iris!' That pleading, like I'm God or maniacal."

Ray said, "If I seek any kind of solidarity from my siblings when I'm in conflict with my parents, immediately it's—it's my fault. And like everything is my problem. Even things I don't start. And since my mother is so conniving she'll often start fights with me and I will get all riled up. And then it's blamed on me. People are pleading with me to stop, everyone starts crying. But it's not even something I started. My mother will start in the most devilish of ways. She'll throw water on me. She'll walk into a room and slap me. And I'll fly into a rage."

The bee returned, landed on Ray.

Ray continued, "And one time I got so pissed at her. Um. And she got so pissed at me. It got physical and she was chasing me around the house and my dog attacked her and then my mom put my dog to sleep the next day."

The bee looked drowsy and still. It liked Ray a lot. Who would not?

"This was when I was in high school. I think it was like my junior or senior year. The dog bit her and my mom ran off to her bedroom crying. And then the next day I come home from school and I'm calling for my dog and my mother comes out of the room almost stoic yet crying at the same time, like this was as much a tragedy for her as it was for me, but she was like: 'Gracie is dead.'"

The sun was going down. Holograms of dead parrots flopped in the road. This was the Good Karma off Pine.

"She named the fucking dog, too. Cause she always wanted to be beautiful like Grace Kelly. So I named the dog Gracie because my mother said she'd always wished she would have named one of her kids Gracie, so I did that as a peace offering when I got the dog, and yeah, she killed it."

The bee moved to the middle of Ray's shirt, tweezing into it and picking at the binder.

"How long will you have to wear a binder still, after surgery?"

"Not long. Maybe five weeks. I was so pissed. I ran away from home. And then I destroyed a bunch of things in our home."

"Like what?"

"I took a golf club and destroyed some of the walls. And then I also kicked holes in some of the walls. This is quite weird, but I took mustard and I deposited streaks and piles of mustard in hard-to-find places, like places she wouldn't find for years. And I think she actually did find them."

You cannot milk a bee for honey. I don't know why I thought that.
I continued. A bee is not a small striped cow.

A cow does not keep its milk in the trees. Shut up.

"She did it while I was at school. And the only thing I had after I
destroyed parts of the house, I was like, 'I'm not going to prom.'
Because my parents were always kind of disgusted by how abnormal
I seemed, so I thought, Ok, this will really hurt them, if I don't do
the normal thing they were banking on—I didn't even want to go
to prom to begin with. Which was so stupid because nobody cared
about me."

A truck pulled in front of Good Karma and huffed there, right
in front of us, causing Ray, who was mostly talking now, to hoarsely
shout their story, and the sun had gone away. There are two Good
Karmas around Pine. This was the one at 22$^{nd}$.

"After the dog thing happened and I'd run away from home I
came back home and I was running a lot. One night I was out for
a run around my block. When I came back my mother was like—a
teacher had called my mother. I had written a poem. A long narrative
poem. For an assignment on *Beowulf*. The teacher called my house
to talk to me about how wonderful, about how extraordinary and
unusual it was and that I should pay attention to writing. But I was
out running and my mother took the call. And when I got back, you
know, she told me all about it: 'I told him you're having a very hard

time right now.' And it was so grotesque to me because I was like, I'm having a hard time right now because you're terrorizing me and you killed my dog."

"What is your relationship like with your family right now?" I asked.

"I feel like I need to stop having contact with any of them. But this is mostly because of how my parents have—I don't know what's going on with them, and I probably will never confront them cause I don't confront them about anything, but ever since I told them I was having surgery they don't talk to me, so. They don't talk to me."

Ray continued. "They don't call me anymore.

"I mean they actually never were that interested in my wellbeing. Like all through grad school they never asked how I was getting by. They never had interest in the kinds of places I was living in. Never visited me once. And my dad did the same thing with this operation. He was into coming and helping me out and then it became clear he did not want to at all. And once that became clear he hasn't talked to me.

"My mother hasn't talked to me at all. The last time I talked to her, which I forget when that was, maybe April, no, maybe March, I don't know, yeah, maybe the end of March because I had already set a date and I'd told her about it and all she said was, 'So that's really happening,' and I was like, 'Yeah,' and she was like, 'Well.' She said something like, 'You better want—This better be something that you want.'

"But neither one of them have called me since. And my dad has started to say things like, 'Well, I don't call you anymore because you put me in a bad mood.' So that has really hurt me. So I might not talk to them ever again. Cause this has been a pattern and I feel like this event is legitimately more serious than the others.

"I have friends who, whenever they have any kind of medical intervention their family rallies behind them. I've never heard of anyone who is shunned for having a medical operation in a city where they know practically no one except for their shitty colleagues, it's just very, I'm not even sure how to interpret it.

"There was a several year period of time during my adolescence. It intersected with the time I was being bat mitzvahed—because I remember thinking at my bat mitzvah: this is a funeral. I was really anorexic.

"To the point of—it was dangerous. My parents took me to a doctor. And that was it. I went to a doctor once. I was doing something wrong and I needed to be punished. Because. I mean this made the whole scapegoating thing a lot worse because I really was sick, but they would constantly call me sick and my sickness was why the family couldn't be a family. And now that word meant two different things because I felt that I was sick actually. They never once treated me with care, like you would treat someone who was in a life-threatening situation. They treated it as a behavioral issue. I don't know how I cured myself of that but I did—once I did, and

41

years after, I've been thinking a lot about that and I think that was maybe the experience I had where I realized I probably shouldn't have anything to do with these people. I can't imagine living with somebody who's helpless and is clearly in immense pain and perhaps going to die and not actually caring how they're doing. Seeing it as a problem. And then that problem would migrate to the outer limits of the family if we ever—we went to Boston again for Thanksgiving and the cousins would ostracize me for ruining everything. 'You need to eat.' It was humiliating.

"Now I feel like I'm going to get laid off while I'm recovering and I'm going to be stuck in a state without the use of my arms. You can't lift something over five pounds for several months after this."

"I didn't know your job was in trouble."

"Of course it is. There are so many lawsuits now. Metal implants cause bad autoimmune reactions."

"I heard of something like that . . ."

"I feel like I need to have this surgery as an event. I need the event to happen because I need a reason to care about myself. Even recovering from it—I need a reason to be gentle to myself. I'm hoping it will unlock something."

Ray was soaking. It had been raining. No, you shouldn't use the rain like that, in your writing. I told students there could be no rain or scenes on benches. Ray was simply, they were crying. They looked so handsome in the rain though. It did not occur to either of us to move inside. The outside seemed so right. The sun had set. The truck was enormous. It was raining in the nighttime, splattering on the metal table. You could see cute things in windows like pianos and shrines.

It occurred to me, "Do you want my house?"

"Iris—you don't mean that. Shut up."

"I should have already mentioned but I'm leaving. I'm getting out of town, like, now. Joe left"—I tapped on my violet hole in the rain—"but you might in the morning switch the locks to be safe."

"I don't have any money for rent."

"Is that yours though?" I pointed at their parking job.

We switched keys and I wished them luck on their surgery.

"When is it exactly?"

"Wednesday. 6 a.m. I'll be out by noon. I can bring everything over to your place beforehand. Then I'll be able to go there after."

I thought about that. I thought about what I was doing. But the letters had retrograded me so hard. And I was sick of these bricks, so many bricks, and worse, the cobblestones on my foot bones. Or the pain spontaneous, anyway, from any angle at all.

"I have to get out of here," I told Ray. I held onto my horrid package. A horse, I felt, stepped on Bouvard who screamed to Péc, "Get out of the way!"

I looked at Ray to see if I could detect that dik-dik look.

/// 

Good Karma was closing down at ten but I got one last little coffee, creamy with lavender, twee, and hopped in Ray's boxy Subaru from the early '90s. It had more than 700,000 miles. It was a matte auburn.

"It's funny seeing a car that's not shiny."

"It's really a town car, you know what I mean? I don't know how far away you'll get."

"Do you want any of these tapes?"

"Where else would I play them? You take them, Iris."

It was a subpar trade, both ways. I told Ray all about the mildew and shadows of my mother's house. But I already knew Ray would spruce it up in a way I couldn't figure out. The shadows would suit their negative affects and then, with their green thumb, they'd make the bathroom's mildew into something more like moss. They'd fashion the toilet into an ancient ruin bewildered with weeds (herbs) and moss, not mildewy. I'd take the car, Gracie II, as far upward as possible. The radiator would be the first thing to smoke, so I'd watch for that. Bouvard and Pécuchet would be very pleased with me. Bouvard would balloon his chest onto the gas as Pécuchet would finally relax, on the left, looking at stars.

"Let's go! Let's go!" Pécuchet sang to Bouvard.

Bouvard shoved and plunged himself on the gas, they were not mad at me any longer. Now that we were going to the country.

It is annoying, though, to leave Philly, you have to get onto a slow bridge no matter what you do, but you don't have to pay (ever) to enter New Jersey. For a long time I drifted on the freeway silent, not really a music lover. Not really. But after peeing at a rest stop up around New York City in the middle of the night, feeling exposed with my often erect nipples in relief in my still raindamp linen jumpsuit, the two of them so available like braille to the words *I* and *Thou*, I went through Ray's tapes near Saugerties.

Ray had in the glovebox and all along the side pockets of Gracie II homemade tapes they'd made in high school, things they'd mixed when they were a teenager and their mom killed Gracie, the dog, for trying to protect them, because the dog wasn't a human. It wasn't disoriented about harm. Here was one tape, though, that had been purchased. A single. It played the same song on both sides.

This was Vivitrix Marigold and the song was titled SCAR. There was very little spool in the tape. It was not a long song. Its tune was part Bikini Kill, a little bit like Hole, and a lot like tracks I'd heard from time to time (very 2000's Tucson) from The Oolong Loon Song System, if you remember her short desert fame, very shouty. There were no musical instruments involved.

I listened to Vivitrix Marigold sing/shout and the radiator smoked. I didn't know how long I had with Gracie II but I did not want to live in New York State. I didn't want to live in or too nearby Albany, so I turned right on a slimmer country lane and sped. There were no dawny rainbows anymore and it got a lot darker. Albany had pushed that morning out earlier, the government, a state government, will do that, stim the cosmos. But the capitol of NY is basically in Vermont, Massachusetts. The country, to the right, was still dark and private and raining a little. I rolled down all of my windows. Cheap joy. Not that cheap if you think about it. A woman alone in a car with a tape is pretty good. The country smelled like manure drinking lavender lattés, like coffee and lavender and shit and smoked milk.

The radiator started to smoke and smoke and smoke. There was a woman from a Rohmer film (the French director) in the engine, who was still in her bed, a bit curled as dictated by the engine parts, and smoking. A smoking woman looks like a person deciding on something, but what is it? What is your decision?

TELL ME.

The woman in bed in the engine was not quick, as she smoked, but the French New Wave scene was cut for speed, something was quick in her languorousness, her decisive ferocity. With all this smoke coming at my window, I thought, I don't have time. Tell me what you have decided. I turned up the volume.

And I listened to that song so many times I could sing to it, and then could sing without the tape playing at all. I stopped playing the tape, which had been like a little training wheel, and I started to sing and shout out SCAR. On repeat. I pushed on through the smoke coming at me. Bouvard was on the gas, leaning his heavy self, so portly, I think he must have been pleased, right onto it, while Pécuchet took some sniffs and held his ears because of the screaming.

"Iris—Iris! We're—going—to—blow—up."

"Hold on, Pécuchet!"

The song began with a long commanding yell—SCAR!

The song had quiet whispering words, and crouching lyrics that always pounced into a big yell. I whispered and screamed the song at COWS!

It went:

SCAR!

I have a scar on my knee
I am sitting there
What is the thing I see
It's not blood anywhere
Because I am SCARRED!
I'm scarred, scarred, scarred, scarred, scarred

I am SCAR!

If I had blood on my knee
From getting hurt badlee

That was, that was
It was a long time AGO! And now I'm SCAR!

I had blood on my knee
I was just sitting there
I had fallen down and on the asphalt arms
Of the WORLD!

The blood was dripping down
The floor was getting so
red, red, red, red, RED!
But now I'm SCAR!

That was a long time ago, that was a long, long, long, long,
    long, long
time AGO!

SCAR! SCAR! SCAR! SCAR!

When I was sitting there
A strange man enterèd
He looked at me but did not see my knee
all dressed in coming blood
He said GET UP!

He said YOU MOVE!

I bled quietlee for a long, long time.
I bled until the blood was mar-i-GOLD!
I bled until my skin was blue, blue scales.
I bled until the scales came OFF!

That was a long
That was a long
That was a very very very very very very long time

Went.

The last word was just, spoken. She just, said it. Went. It was just, very dramatic. Just, just, that sick, overly warm word, ENOUGH! The song was not too great on paper, fine, but you'd have to hear it or try yourself to sing it out in order to see the brilliance of VM. The sun was rising. Pécuchet was holding his ears and whimpering by the end, so very annoyed and withered, when we arrived, like, poof, when the car died absolutely. It went.

"You think you're alone in the country, Iris—there are people though sleeping in those houses," said Pécuchet, with bitterness but, you could tell, *exuberance*.

Bouvard hopped first from Gracie II, totally dead, and up in some smoke as if we had appeared here by ordinance of a spell.

Pécuchet wanted me to never sing that song to them or anyone or even to myself ever again. He truly pleaded: "It's not attractive. It's not pleasing. I don't like it."

I smiled. Then I had the car towed to a nearby mechanic and sold it for a very few of its parts ($200) and dried myself out in the sunshine, on a BENCH.

**PART 2 / VIVITRIX MARIGOLD IN THE COUNTRY**

A cow was stepping on my, Vivitrix's, heart and I could feel her—the weight.

I was lying in the grass. I had not eaten or taken shelter in a few days. You are supposed to fast, I'd heard, to reset the immune system. My dark-green shoes were so dark against the higher greens of summer grass they'd turned blacklooking, and looked platinum or like black maryjanes because of the dew, because they were shining.

It was very early, it was five in the morning. That's so early. I had fallen asleep on a hill that emptied itself down to The mARTin. I had fallen asleep but I don't know for how long.

This kind of museum. That gets attention for being out in the middle of a New England nowhere, so not *that* nowhere. Not poor. No, this was all richie rich. This kind of museum, I mean, that is remote but at the center of money, has a haj-like aura about it for a certain type of scholar of money, I mean people like New Yorkers who make an arty annual pilgrimage, wafting around the grounds—sculpture garden, an outdoor pop-up orchestra—in white linen tunics looking a lot like modernist rheumatologists looking at something, at art, with squid pins, or something, brill with rhinestones, these things in their messy, I don't know, Swissish hair.

Before The mARTin—before I can even get into all of that—lay a half acre of black marble harboring a good deal of flat balsamic water so that the museum was looking down at itself, static and at a slant.

I felt too close for comfort to the narrator of "The House of Usher"—eeeee—who views, in that famous Poe story, the house of his old school friend Usher only first through a *tarn* that glosses it.

The narrator looks first only at the tarn, not at the formidable house, which peers *itself* into the tarn like an enormous cracked narcissist. The house has, if you remember, an infamous crack, and this truly comes to a head later when it falls apart.

Like that narrator, that man, so too I, Vivitrix, first looked at the reflective water rather than at a real building, weird, so I first saw The mARTin upside down. Its pink door stretched tall on morning's mandible, as though it were flocked in flamingo leather, a pink surpassing the high heat of "hot," a flamingo ultravinegar spilled all over something like a primed bookcover of a welcome new monograph on someone like Sade, or Wilde, someone such as Rimbaud or O'Hara, or Keats, men with honorary vaginas who were castrated by love and the system, Flaubert, Adorno or Baldwin. It was a *very* hot pink door.

Ok I get it, I thought, The mARTin is importantly insouciant. It's importantly not straight. But was it?

In the reflective pool I also saw, though cut off by the beginning of grass, some Helvetic metal letters, which were bolted to the museum's flat clean-lined roof on little sturdy stilts and were the purest version I'd ever seen of marigold (my new surnamesake), so that these letters must, I thought, integrate strangely with a sunrise or -set. Probably, I thought, it looks like letters are coming right out of it when the sun does set, or if you sat on the hill like this and watched it set, it sets, you'd see these metal marigold *pieces*—legs and arms—bobbing out of the endlessly ending sun.

The sun develops *as* it ends. The color gets so stabby.

I read these letters backwards at first, but I can read backwards if I apply myself even a little bit. And so there was I, Vivitrix Marigold, at The mARTin. Art in emphasis. Kind of cheesy.

A *tarn* is a cold mountain lake.

The mARTin appeared to be built with wood, the material of many a New England clapper, but like the reflecting pool it was also marble. With gravely etched indents to create that visual trick of slats. Its hot pink door was remarkably very small, like the door to a regular house tacked onto the wrong kind of place. This was obviously an institution, not a home. It was closed up, too. Signs at half-acre marks all around this land:

SUMMER IS OUR RESTING PERIOD.
A TIME TO CREATE AND CURATE.
*TO REFLECT*.
WE'LL SEE YOU SOON.

This cow was still stepping on me. I really couldn't believe it. But it didn't even hurt. I wondered at my strength. Wow. She had a scar all across her udder, a crusty violet line. Maybe recent? Her udders swayed like a too wholesome chandelier. Maybe she did not know she was stepping on a person. I didn't want her to move, startled or dumbly, and step her foot onto my face or throat. My heart was a hard-enough platform for this problem, but what else on me could take it?

I watched dung plop to my feet.

How do you *think* they felt?

They had been at it all night, so I had hardly slept. Pécuchet was particularly hard to please, so anxious he was, always, about his artistic output. Pécuchet was so insecure. Bouvard soothed him, but it wasn't his forte. I'd rubbed them in some promising looking weeds (herbs) and secured on them bonnets of stolen cabbage, which is honestly good for inflammation. But the world vibrated with pain. I woke up from its pain, and had to listen all night to these men:

"Bouvard, I'm silly—a fool."

"Pécuchet, now now, you are God's silly fool."

"Oh, I'm conniving."

"You have a vision!"

"Bouvard, this so-called medication has ruined all of my focus and my neural synapses are completely shot—I can't think, I can't write . . . I hate what she takes."

He was referring to the low doses of chemo I took for my arthritis and which I'd left at the house on Naudain St. So it wasn't going to be a problem.

"Dear Pécuchet, you are only writing from a vessel that's working best as it can, and maybe anyway all of that hyperconnectivity you remember so nostalgically needed to, you know, take a bow."

"Bouvard, you don't realize. You like me, but I am not fundamentally likable, so what I write can't ultimately be communicable."

"Really, Pécuchet. You are a beautiful trying soul and anyone can see that!"

"I can be very lazy . . ."

"Energy needs to be played calmly and tactically."

"Bouvard?"

"Yes?"

"What is writing for?"

"Oh Lord. Take heart, take heart, writing is the writing on your heart."

"Idiot. I feel for you. My writing cannot possibly matter."

"I can't sleep. Who knows what's going to happen now. Your writing is not alone, Pécuchet. It's with all of the other writing, so go to sleep."

But Pécuchet stayed up. Bouvard slumbered. They could not ever sleep together, in concert. My left foot simply hurt too much. It would not stop simply hurting, and throbbing, which is when sobbing goes swinging, when it hangs upside down above poison.

When Pécuchet slept, when he'd finally got calm, Bouvard woke up reeling, his spine whipping him like this big whip of bones. My right foot honestly felt like it was breaking in two, right there in the grass. Sheetless, the moon glazing my body in its séance. I wanted to die. What was I going to do, carry my feet with me on my shoulder like two pet rats? Was I going to be that guy, but a woman with her two feet?

Frustrated, and too hot, the old retired men had already thrown their anti-inflammatory bonnets away from them in the grass. Now this. Both of them having dung slopped, wet and dripping, on their arches. Are there healing properties in cow dung? A sick person peers at the natural world convulsively, aching. Pécuchet screamed and wailed:

"Oh! Oh! Why! Why!"

"You wanted to leave Paris," I thought to them. It was in their mouths, between my toes. Dung. And the cow would not stop standing on me. The udders dribbled milk on my face and on my jumpsuit, making it paler, buttercupping its bitter color with what the second-wave feminist Hélène Cixous called her "white ink." Oh god. She treated breastmilk like a white metaphor, a loose glue, white, a summer soup of female outputs. Ink on tap. But you can't write inside of the bodies of babies. You can't open infants like a book, not without a terrible amount of malice.

Dairy is very inflammatory and I hadn't been this close to real milk in months. I would have rather drunk blood, I confess, I'd have rather drunk from a dairy cow's neck or eaten her shit off of my hurting feet than drink even a momentary dribble from a giving udder. I had my special diet to consider. But my heart was doing great. It didn't even feel hard up, the hoof merely using it as a kind of dais. I only cried out because milk dribbled on my lips.

I deliberated as to whether or not I should, though, scream.

"Vivitrix," Bouvard called up, "if you do not find a rag, if we do not take a bath . . ."

My phone rang nearby me.

"Do not answer that now!" wailed Pécuchet. "Can you believe her?" he whimpered to Bouvard.

I said it was an ok time to speak and where the fuck was he?

"Where the fuck are *you*? I'm back at the house, with Ray?"

"What? You came back?"

"But Ray lives here now?"

Bouvard interrupted, "Vivitrix, can you please handle this all later?"

"Are you all right? Where did you go?"

"I'm ok, Babe. I got myself to some meetings. Everything is ok. Ray had a surgery so I'm helping them with their drains? They're, like, attached to them."

"Oh. Are they in ok spirits?"

"Iris, where are you? Don't you need to go teach today? Who are you with?"

The cow was not alone. It was with tens of other cows on this hill above The mARTin. You could see them all, if you looked down into the black marble pool. They mottled there on top of the museum in an overlay of reflection. The clouds lay over the cows and museum. The sun was a crystal pit overlaying everything almost like a moon, cleanshaven of any rays or outreach. The cows were all brown and white and black. The one stepping dumbly, aloofly, on me was chocolate brown like a bison. It was high time she stepped off of me. I could give you, you cow, a papercut, I bitterly thought. That's all I really had to give. I took out my two letters. I wondered which one she wanted. The one from when I was fourteen was worse, because I was younger, but the one when I was sixteen, that one sounded much meaner. They were very very cutting. Where was the first one? Let's see . . .

Joe said, "Iris. Iris."

What did he want?

"Ray won't tell me where you went. I don't think they know? Their drains get so full, like forty cc's by seven every night. I empty them out. I don't think they're supposed to fill that much though, Babe. Ray says their body is fighting with a loss it doesn't understand and so fills up with fluids. I think they got tumors out or something? Why would your body fight so much with that? Hey good riddance, right, Iris?"

I could not imagine any of this. Joe, helping someone . . .

"I don't want to say where I am at the moment," I said.

The cow pressed harder into me, like she was leaning down for deeper grass. My heart felt like it was touching my back. No, it was buried beneath me.

"Let's meet. I can meet you wherever you are. Or let's meet up next week in Tucson. I'll get on a plane."

"Be honest. Are you taking Ray's Oxycontin?"

"That's all right, Iris, I have plenty of my own stuff to take."

Did Joe mean the stuff I had left? Would Joe really want to take chemo? He liked a lot of drugs. He was born so obsessed with everything. And so goodlooking. And sure, he would often take the syringes I used to push the chemo into me every Friday evening, as I used the weekend to be the most sick. A lot of people do it like that. He took those syringes when I was done with them, what restraint, looking at me like a dog while I took it, waiting for his stupid stick.

"Have fun with chemo—I don't care."

"All right I did take some of Ray's pills, but, Iris, they say they're fine with it. A lot of people don't mind this stuff. They don't love so conditionally. They don't even care. It's helping me focus, so I can help with the drains."

"What about Tucson? Would you have any money to get on a plane?"

Pécuchet absolutely lost it. He said, "FUCKING ENOUGH. We didn't retire to the goddamn country to have Joe dog the trip, Iris—I mean Vivitrix. Do not say where we are. Do not. And wipe this dung from my mouth and eyes. No, it's not possible. If you go, we're not coming."

I miss him, I thought. I said, "There's nothing we can do here. The museum's not even open."

"She misses him already," Bouvard sighed.

"He's a louse. I've seen him be a louse!" wailed Pécuchet. He put his own foot in his mouth and bit it open.

"Iris, would you get my ticket?" asked Joe, but I hung up in some pain. If you turned this scene on its side, I was getting tacked to the hill, hanging there, like a human painting. And udders hung down on me like a wholesome microphone system. Milk fell into my mouth as I began to read my dad's first letter out loud:

"Dear Kenneth and Iris,

This Father's Day will be devastating for me if I cannot be with you."

I could not quite keep reading. I was shaking in the grass like an Etch-a-Sketch a higher power was trying to erase wholesale. Fuck that. I stopped shaking. My feet stopped shaking. No one is shaking, so stop.

My heart was free. It suddenly ended. Things suddenly end. No one understands unless, until they get sick. Then they'll see how unruly it is, how outside of help. It's more like entering a tunnel of prayer. But the cow did take herself off of me. It felt like the release of a young lantern. An octopus is born. Did the reading of my letter repel her? I hadn't even gotten to anything really smart. The part that was so mean. No, it wasn't because of me.

Someone else had said, "Get OFF!"

Then that cow got off and went away uphill. That's it. I hadn't thought of speaking as a potential area for helping myself. A scapegoat does not believe, and I'll say this twice, that *anything* coming out of her mouth can be heard. Not without SCREAMING. Not without a trick. It does not work to say, This hurts. It does not work to say, Please. But I had not even thought to say anything at all. I thought, All right, death by hoof. Yes. A scapegoat doesn't think she can ask. No, she doesn't believe in honest questions.

I could not believe I was alive after all. I'll never eat beef again, I promise, I thought. But I had often thought this, in many different encounters with cattle, like when you look at a cow, when it looks at its calf, when its calf looks at you, when sunstreams pleat in a hermeneutics of fear and tenderness, and you say, I'll never.

A cow's eyeball, what is that? Warmest stone struck by lightning, fluidic, no, a perfect ball, the pit, each one, of a perfect brown and shining pond. They wore these pond-pits in their concerned faces.

A cow is very concerned for her calf, I've seen as much. A cow is never wild, it's not possible. There are no wild cattle, though deer, I've heard, are the cattle of witches? But I would eat a cow—beef, and venison, too. I knew as much. I'd eliminated all gluten and dairy and grains, and starch, because they made my bones crack like a house, and I needed some beef like you wouldn't beleef.

"Hello?"

I sat up, my feet full of shit. Starving.

"Was she stepping on you? Did she step right on you?"

"For a while . . ."

"I'm so sorry, they are heart-stepping cows. They've been trained to find and step on people's hearts in the grass, through the generations, though they don't ever apply any pressure. Thank god. They arrived yesterday from this tiny town in Germany, Sachsenhausen. Have you heard of it? There's a concentration camp there, it's outside of Berlin. I don't mean one of the current ones, it's not in operation, it's a touristic area. These are the last of this heritage herd and we got them at auction last month, but we haven't even been able to see what they really do. Until just now, I saw you under her. Did that hurt?"

"She wasn't really applying pressure, you're right."

"Well, they used to do that at the dairy farm in the hill above the camp in Sachsenhausen. People would escape and lie in the tall grass. These cows, really their ancestors, would come step on any heart still beating and wait there until the farmer came and shot them. I mean the person. So that's why she was doing that to you, to help this SS-compliant farmer. Or that legacy is in her, is the point. She doesn't do that for anyone, but the breed couldn't shake the gesture, at all, and you could—I guess up until now—go to Sachsenhausen and lie in the field for a good heart-stepping, and the farmer's great-granddaughters were advertising it, making it something fun for the kids. But then this American kid died because he had a very weak heart to begin with and it was like stepping on warm butter with all of his problems. They should never have let him under her. People there, in Sachsenhausen, turned quickly against the herd because they are solely devoted to the tourism the camps bring, which relies on death being *over* and the camps being a monument to a death that isn't really possible anymore, but here was death, here was this boy who dies right on the nose of the Holocaust, skewered onto its nose by this ancestral hoof?

65

"They were going to kill the cows for this—at last—but they were auctioned instead. You know how it goes. A Spanish artist we admire very much was there anyway, in Sachsenhausen, at the residency space for artists that is there. It's right in town, on a block before the camps. It's a prime location, on a camp block. Irina contacted us immediately saying she wants to do something for us with these cows, an exhibit, in early September. We only do one thing for one month—September—so it's high stakes around here, but we love Irina and have been watching and cultivating her, so we authorized her to buy the herd at auction for whatever amount, and it is amazing how much of our money now pumps and plashes in the town of Sachsenhausen, to the granddaughters of this SS farmer's daughters and to the commission on tourism and perhaps in part to the international artist residency there, which is really a house belonging to an officer who directed much of the daily work at the concentration camp, so a fine bourgeois German home with his library still in use for the artists, lots of Goethe, you can imagine, a shelf devoted only to fine editions of that novel *Elective Affinities*, etcetera. It's very international and competitive to go there, and Irina goes almost every year. She practically summers in Sachsenhausen, and we love her. I love her instincts, and we always want her to come here again and do something amazing, so she bought these heart-stepping cows at any price and we had them shipped on a barge actually to Boston, and then they were picked up and driven west. They're very tired and, I think, seasick, but you can see they are already happy. This was always supposed to be a farm, in fact it *was* a dairy farm, though Martin, my husband, had no interest in maintaining that. We never really, when he was alive, grafted to the land. I would say we were almost against it.

"It's been a total mess getting them here, and Matthew only got back last night because he doesn't fly, so he has to take boats. He takes an ocean liner, and I think he wanted Irina to come with him, but she was insulted or perhaps repulsed. She said she didn't want to plow like that through water. She said the air is the right weight for movement. I think she thought she was being asked out, like propositioned, so I had to tell her Matthew's asexual. But we're flying her here, routing her back through Spain. She says she needs a week to recover in Spain after being immersed in the camps in Germany. She says she goes around visiting the royal gardens in Seville. She says, she's dramatic, I love her, 'Caroline, I need to be driven over back and front by big flowers to get the camps off,' as if flowers take the wheel of a car, can you imagine? That big goofy lily just honking and crashing into you, in what kind of car? A toad-skinned Fiat— beep beep! We love Irina. We can't wait to see her. At first I thought you were her—you look like her—but who are you? You know we only open for September? That's it. And we only do one exhibition. It's high stakes, I know. Though now that I think of it, what are we going to do? These cows probably need more than grass, right? I

67

thought I could just empty them out onto our land, from the trucks, and there you are, roam, eat. Take shits wherever, it's called dung, I don't care. But do they need to be milked, do you think? Is it a matter of their relief? Look, you're all covered in milk. They probably need that, to be milked. But I don't know."

I took a deep breath. You have to manage up. You have to work.

"I can do that if you want."

"You're a tender of cows?"

"A cowherd, yes."

"Sorry. Excuse me. You look more like Irina than a cowherd. Irina is really cool and beautiful. I'm probably just in love with her."

Caroline asked me to come down to the museum to fill out paperwork. I put my shitty feet into my shining black shoes. What a mess.

She seemed sixty, with red and silver hair in a very large and particularly ebullient bun, a balloon of a stormcloud of tight curls and helium with its string tied invisibly around her neck. This big bun bobbed almost directly above her head, like she used helium in her hair products. This precious-metal bun of red-gold and silver, of frizz and dazzle, was nice.

She wore black athleisure and was tall and totally tawny with big jagged freckles coming together into auburn tarns on her very muscular arms. She seemed mountainous, sure, not that she had large breasts or even large or particularly feminine curves, but she seemed to be like a system. She seemed, to me, so orogenous.

It occurred to me, Vivitrix, she was the kind of person who looks *so good*. If she looked sixty years old, she might *be* eighty or ninety-five.

We were inside now, past the long clean lines of the empty museum, into an upstairs englassed office, but it had once been their family home.

"When my husband died," said Caroline, "Matthew said to me: 'Mom, when a dad dies, a house becomes like a museum,' and we just went with it. Lord knows we had an influx of cash."

"I can't quite imagine this as a house."

"You use that word, *quite*."

"A teacher I loved used it, so now I do."

"You had a love affair with your teacher?"

"No, I only loved her. Quite."

"Oh. Well, this area is very beautiful, it's the country. And Martin wanted a house that was like a big brick of money. This place is all internally striped in gold, inside all the marble of the walls. The house itself is like a safe, he was very concerned about the economy. He didn't trust the digitization of cash. He worked with student loans though, very much a materialist."

Behind Caroline there was a large painting that looked like an actual Renoir, one of that Impressionist painter's later more fucked out works, a nude (of course) with smaller blushing breasts, but with the bigger rougher strokes signature of his decline. He painted, late in life, with a beaked hand, the paintbrush being strapped to it by a nurse, so it was not confidence, this late sensual style—some called it genius—but the risen froth of a circumstance.

"Did you know," Caroline said, "the poor painter had rheumatoid arthritis, really bad?"

She tapped on the painting, roughly, the way you'd treat your own dog.

The top of it had been treated—this was clear—with a powerhose hooked to a vat of turpentine, so a Twomblish rainfall struck through the girl. Wasn't a painting like this worth millions of dollars?

"Matthew just hates Renoir," Caroline continued. "I bought this for his last birthday, to do whatever he wanted with. Like buying a torture doll, you know?"

No, I, Vivitrix, had never heard of that . . .

"I didn't know what he would do! There are a lot of things around, it's like Clue around here, that game? There's a gun, a rope, some poison? But I think he did something really artistic and that's great. And then he gave it to me, for my own birthday, which was yesterday. Right before he slumped off with his infamous *days* long boat-lag. When will Matthew even emerge!"

"What birthday was it?"

"You mean how old am I?"

"Or Matthew. I'm curious."

"He's not someone you'd date. He's not really asexual, what I told Irina, but you know, he's quite—to use your expression—*quite* Heathcliffish."

I was signing all these forms to become the cowherd. There was no health insurance. I didn't know anything, where I'd live. I felt I might die of hunger as I signed: Vivitrix Marigold.

"I have often thought, Pécuchet, that my own rectum was like a big baggy stigmata," mused Bouvard.

"I have thought the same . . ."

"We must find out more of the details surrounding Christ's death, and his life!"

"If only for a scientific purpose, to understand more about what the body could endure in, say, a medical procedure."

"But wasn't his death voluntary? That's how it's always put, he died *for* us. Is that not true?"

"What does it mean actually to cure? Don't you cure something if it hangs like that, left out and dead in the air?"

"No, no, *salt* cures, or sugar. Air is not a component of curing, when we speak of meats. But they did *preserve* him. But did they throw salt onto him? Did they, at all as they took life, spice him? No, I believe it was rocks, but if the rocks were salty rocks or rocks of desert salts it is possible . . ."

"Murder was not so odd, you can't think so for those times. Murder here, murder there. Other people, too, were strung up like that as well, with frequency! On many crosses all around, I suppose . . . But it was such a slow murder, Bouvard. Think of that. It lasted for how long? Is patience to be so admired? Is patience, too, cruel? But I wonder, Bouvard, if really this was the birth of the concept of a process?"

They said *process* kind of British. Pro-sess.

"Process comes from the slow murder of Jesus. I like that, Pécuchet. I like that a lot. We have to do something with that, here in the country."

"Everything must have an origin if even process has an original sin. We must trace everything back so diligently. Oh, we are cut out for some work."

"We'll work. We'll study. Now that we are finally here."

"Come with me," Caroline said, "into the old kitchen. I'll make you an omelet before you get out there."

"Is there not to be a bath!" Bouvard shouted up. Bouvard, Pécuchet. I loved them. But, you know, I looked down on them.

"It's not clear," said Caroline, "that the command to have a family is any different than the command to kill your family." She'd changed. She was getting down to some sort of business.

We were in a kitchen in the basement. They did their living either underneath or above the museum, even though it was only such a thing for a month, god knows why. This kitchen was large, white, modernist, with a wide refrigerator that looked like a convincing part of the cabinetry. When Caroline opened it a pink light, like that which dawns on a fuchsia incline in a James Turrell room (artist of colored lights), appeared, and she explained, "James is a friend."

She took out eggs, tahini, lemons, and bacon from what seemed a refrigerating sunset. She took out some champagne.

"To working with us! To the heart-stepping cows of Sachsenhausen!"

We toasted. It was not even 9 a.m.

"The command to have a family is not different than the command to kill your family?"

Caroline tried to explain this concept. "If you can imagine, Vivitrix, we are always so horrified when we hear about—we are necessarily horrified when we hear about fathers or estranged fathers or let's say these persons who are occupying the position of the father. They are carrying the intensity, they are carrying the symbolic unity of the family in all of its ambivalence, and then they destroy their families. These fathers slaughter their families. They murder their families."

"It does seem to pop up in the news quite often. Not in the main headlines in *The New York Times* or *L.A. Times* or like that, but somewhere in the slew of freakish events reported online, this story —a father kills everyone—is very persistent."

"There's an equivalent of this, of course, in maternal psychosis. It's only that it seems to me that at the same time as we are saying 'Have the family and therefore reconstitute the universe,' we are also saying, 'Murder the family and break from the universe because you can't do it and it's too much.' Those two things kind of come together, and it feels to me that in the arc of American civilization at this moment we've never been more openly ambivalent about those things, such that the ethos of care and the ethos of abuse begin humming together and producing a third harmony that is reducible perhaps neither to the family nor to murder but might be opening on a generalized psychosis of the social field."

Caroline was doing a maddeningly slow scramble—very French—on her eggs. She had set the heat so low. Bouvard and Pécuchet twitched. The eggs were not even halfway towards a soft curd. I was upset. My stomach shook from hunger. My poor stomach was to become, at this rate of egg cookery, sprung by pain, a whole other character in this story of revenge. The revenge of the scapegoat.

Caroline continued to explain, "So whatever the family is, Vivitrix, I think it is a place that begins to produce a kind of separating harmonic. We can no longer be together in the mode of the family. Or in order to do so, when we do enter into it, everyone acknowledges at some level that it's basically unbearable? Right, there's something so crazy about it. A person's daily life will become perfumed with this language, 'I love it, but they make me crazy,' 'I love it, but I can't do it.' 'I love it, but I'm completely exhausted all of the time.' So you're forced to say both things. That you love it more than anything but that it's killing you. *That* is the degree zero of being in it. Many things are like that, of course."

"You talk about the father and mother, what about the murderous child in the family? You see that a lot. And I can personally think of a few times when I wanted to kill everyone in my family. Of course, I wanted to kill myself, too."

I was remembering, specifically, what Kenneth once did to a box.

There had been a box, and it did not have any branding on it like other boxes for cigars. My box was of a wooden brown maybe made in somebody's workshop, with, as you are imagining, the traditional little golden clasp. I don't know where I'd found it.

"What was the earliest time you felt like destroying your own family?"

"At eight or nine. My brother, Kenneth, wanted a box that I kept in my bedroom. He did not covet it, but he wanted to use it for something at school. The box seemed, to him, to come from an era his class, or maybe it was even the whole school, was going to reconstruct—what era could it have been? The box was incredibly simple and unmarked. I have no idea where it came from."

"So he stole your box?" The eggs were not cooked. Caroline stirred them continuously, breaking up the heating process, stretching heat into so much minutiae. She even took the pan entirely off the stove and walked around the kitchen with it, stirring and cooling this hardly stiffening buttercuppish soup.

The yolks were very pale, store bought I guess, but no, she had not added any milk. Phew.

"No, Kenneth requested that he be allowed to use it, to me first and then—I refused—to our parents. This was a box in which I kept leaves, stones, stickers, the assortment of things that have importance, and a prism was in my box that I would hold up—I'd fill it up like getting oil, like my bedroom window in the morning was this rainbow refilling station, I'd cup this prism and hurry it back into the box every single day, restoring rainbows into its internal and incredibly humble dimension, like a philosopher's hut was this amazing box, this terrarium of my private science."

Caroline clarified, "It could be the child who destroys the family. Anyone could take up this command, sure. But earlier I was more saying this was like a bifurcating narrative, but I don't think it's a bifurcation because a bifurcation assumes there's a point of tension. A crisis intervenes, like your box, and then there's a split. That would be like a psychodynamic model of these things. There's psychological preconditions, a crisis befalls, the bifurcation happens—I'm not suggesting that."

She was serious on this point.

She turned off the stove entirely. She turned it off. She set down the pan and whisked tahini with squeezes of lemon and warm water.

76

The kitchen had one window, a joke, the view was soil. Above the sink worms trawled, red and flat from the glass. Where did they think they were?

She continued, "I'm more suggesting, Vivitrix, that there's a simultaneity of realities working along one another. I guess that is kind of a bifurcation but it's slipperier and weirder and more dangerous than there just being psychological preconditions that then enable this explosive act of violence—killing your family.

"It is more like that explosive unthinkable act of violence is there and is *equally normative*, and it has as much of a command, and we *want* it as much as we want the family. It's a death drive that is in its own way productive, and it's not just annihilating, right, it's like *constructing a sacrifice*, or it's constructing the sacrifice *of itself*. There is a command that comes, and you can hear a mixed music in it, and it is both 'Have this thing' and 'Destroy this thing.' And how do you be at peace with that?

"There's all kinds of internal traps and very cruel acts of signification, kinds of deductions of violence that are built into this notion of the family that are very grotesque if you assume that it's all you can do. But it's not like we're given—I'm making it sound like it's a matter of agency. You're not going to do a Cartesian reconstitution of your free will in these moments. I think in a way you have to—at least as a thought experiment—assume that you can relate to things in a different way."

Caroline offered me nothing. She had no mothering in her actual

77

way. No coffee, no water. No ink as white as a breast's divulgence. Whatever. She was clean of things. Even the champagne had been trifling, now was entirely put away. She was making me a breakfast I did not any longer believe in. These were some show eggs. She was all endless prosess, pro-sessing, murderous patience, and I'd die.

"By the way, what is that package? You're clutching onto it so hideously. Irina would never clutch like that. She's really calm. I love her, she's so certain. I keep asking her back here, keep wanting more of her."

"I can't get into my package right now." Dying . . . of . . . hunger . . .

"Ok then tell me more about your box. What was so significant about it that it made you want to destroy your family, perhaps for the first time?"

"My brother requested he take this box into his school to use for the project, right. I said, 'No, definitely no.' But it fit the bill in some way, for the era his school was discovering, and so my parents commanded me to empty out my box and hand it over."

"And you did that?"

"Of course. What options did I have? I removed everything from the box, and everything that was once inside of it trembled on my shelf, naked and questioning me."

"You could have destroyed the box. You might have irresolvably immolated it, I would think. So was the agreement that the box should be returned to you ever?"

"It was agreed I could have the box back, as soon as Kenneth was done with using it at his school."

"Kenneth sounds fine."

"No! No, he's not fine! They made me disband my box. They watched me as I pulled a prism like a fossilized angel's annulus right out of it, all the while whispering to it. I was delirious. A scapegoated child wears a coat of many whispers."

"The scapegoat, I see."

"Yes, and it plagues me. I still whisper. I whisper a lot in my song, SCAR!"

"Oh, a recording? You must sing it for us, whenever Matthew emerges. That is a mystery. And when Irina lands. I can't wait."

She took down a very large and entirely flat black plate. It felt like a warning, this eclipsish ceramic. But the starved, as you know, would eat off of an eclipse. Sure. She put the eggs back on the stove and turned it on, to even a low medium. You don't know what that did to my heart.

"All I'm really saying, Vivitrix, is that for many subjects it becomes impossible to distinguish between 'Now I'm the anchor of a world for others in a particular way,' and then also having to destroy that world. You can be in that position and it's impossible to distinguish between those two tasks. Or even, the way you hold it is that you realize that your obligation is actually to destroy your family, or to take the thing down. I often wonder if something like that is operating *not* as the background, not as the secret obscene thing, but that's just *what it is*? Can we even tell the difference between those—do we even know the difference between those two things? We know it after the fact, and we say—someone kills their family— it's a tragedy and a nightmare, but, it seems like something—it's like, it's not even *reality* that's manifesting, it's like another fold of this fan, of this texture that we're already woven into and whose pieces we experience linearly while in fact it's already continuous, we're already on a pleated surface."

She gave me food. She put it on that really flat plate. But she was looking, for some time, for a clean fork. My fingers shook.

"But what about the suicide part?"

"Well, they often go together, murder, suicide, Vivitrix. You become a suicidal subject insofar as you're part of this group enunciation. So it's not just about deleting yourself from the circuit, though for many people perhaps it is, but no, there's a kind of circuit of shared will that I guess from the perspective I'm trying to enunciate absolutely has a kind of ramified series of belongings, and the individual pieces aren't necessarily extricable from it. There's like, *whatever you are*, presumably. Your family. The society. Blah blah blah. Your vision of unity. But they all contain one another. So there's a series of these part-to-whole relationships. Once you're in there, you can't just subtract pieces out of it. It's not really modular in that sense. It's also not escaping to do a murder-suicide either. In a way that also is normative. So we're in a scenario where there isn't really a pathological case of exception. I would say that whatever the secret of our socius is, *we also are suiciders*, or families that become suicides, or suicides that were always a family. That's just one of the things we do. It's not necessarily an aberration. It is part of our practice."

"So did you kill Martin?"

"How can you say that? Did you kill your parents? No, but you were sensitive, weren't you? A child's fingers are very sharp like a demon's. They can pierce into things, especially stones. You, I mean the adults, have to defend whatever these kids are touching. You have to watch for what they really touch. If you looked at the bottom of that prism, you'd see something like a scar where you'd inserted (really stuffed in) almost all of yourself. And your mother at that time was so sick, and so tired and in bed, right? That box was much better than her to you. It was being better to you at that time. And Kenneth took it with him to his school."

"Did I say anything about a sick mother?"

What was this? Who was Caroline? Was this telepathy or irrealism? No, no, I'd been to the bathroom. Right.

I should have remembered that I went to the bathroom. I should have *mentioned* the bathroom.

81

I had told students earlier in Philadelphia, at the arts college, when I had posed in that teacherly manner, "Of course your characters have gone to the bathroom at some point, but your reader doesn't need to know everything that happens or in order. But whoever you're writing about, they probably excused themselves at some point to collect themselves and to pee or empty their bowel and marvel at soaps, but in fiction you don't say everything unless you're a man."

I was pissed.

The bathroom is a sanctuary to the adult scapegoat, it's still a holy closet, it still has that door with a lock. What a good place to gather oneself and to exhale liquid and to exhale even excrement, there is no such thing as an unlockable bathroom, not in society.

I told them, "Of course your characters are going to the bathroom. But you can't tell your reader every little thing that happens, that's not even realism. So you have to decide if it's significant that they go and do that."

And at the time I really didn't think it was, that I went. I didn't know Caroline would snoop through my things, and I didn't want to be strange, carrying my package with me to the toilet as though it contained some kind of custom toilet paper for my oblong anal vagina, or drugs.

No, I didn't want her to think her new cowherd was addicted.

I told my students as I adjuncted my bold heart out, "When you write, make it a personal goal that this writing becomes something that goes to live in a bathroom. Not many objects have that opportunity. Towels, soap, of course, maybe some shells and jewels. Not that many. Think of the bathroom. Think of what that is for you, and for others. That lock. That haven. That little office of so much mercy. Society's only redeeming feature and it's almost worth it, all this pain, if you could live like that in there. If you, by the proxious ear of your writing, are pulled in there, if you live by someone's toilet in a hamlet all of porcelain, that is a grand grand life and a better honor than a review of your work in *The New York Times* or in *The New Yorker*, which is where the poet John Updike held a desk for many years . . ."

I said to Caroline, "Wait. What? Did you read my dad's letters? You snooped me?"

"Yes. Only one of them, the first thing that came out, when you went to the bathroom."

I had gone to the bathroom.

I'd excused myself from her englassed office upstairs. I had not done a lot of things in a while so I did everything in there. It was so white and serene. The lock was a bolt. There was a fan giving a lush amount of privacy. The soap was in the shape of a hot pink crab's claw, it reached for me. It was milled sage, and the soaking tub, not in use, was clotted with potted plants. On the wall were true Picasso sketches, such as the one titled "Sleeping Nude and Man Writing," in which a man writes (probably everything that ever happened) next to a splayed and hairy slit as the nude is asleep in a very available way, very fungible and prehensile.

Behind these was this custom wallpaper, made particularly for The mARTin, a repeating print of *New York Times* reviews for many of the different openings in the ten years or so since the death of Caroline's husband. So since it opened.

The reviews were dated September 1st, very prompt, so I could tell The mARTin really had *The New York Times* in its claw, and this specialty wallpaper covered everything up to even the year previous when Irina was in the spotlight. Bold move. Irina one year and then the next. Maybe Caroline really was in love with her. But in any case they were cultivating her arduously—and she'd bought the year previous (no doubt with Caroline's $$$) Frida Kahlo's diary from the Coyoacán museum in Mexico. Frida! Anything Frida! An easy sensation for any museum. But *The New York Times* reports that Irina Olín revised the diary by re-painting directly onto it (Kahlo used paint as her writing ink)—"'Diego, Diego,' the diary keeps up its chant, a monoagriculture (useless) of a name (a man) she was obsessed with"—now it read, in Irina's red paint, DIABLO.

The *Times* ends on approval, "One may flinch at this, a young Spanish artist defiling the precious work of Mexico's Kahlo, but the attack is closer to a defense for this disabled artist who lay in her work-bed constantly painting that name Diego—*Mi Diego, ya no estoy sola*—while what did he care, that asshole?"

The review continued in its astutions, "The writer Carlos Fuentes, who introduces Kahlo's diary in the print edition, aptly anoints her as a symbol for a century worth of pain and torture: 'Frida Kahlo is one of the greatest speakers for pain in a century that has known, perhaps not more suffering than other times, but certainly a more unjustified and therefore shameful, cynical and publicized, programmed, irrational, and deliberate form of suffering than ever.'"

The *Times* (which transmogrifies the whole wary world into bait) called this unappealing Spanish conquest—see the review's cute, clickbait title "Hasta 'Diego,' Baby"—"art in the intertext," and Irina Olín used, of course, *of course*, her period blood. Who would not?

It's terrible not to use something that is colorful and abundant and is cosmic insofar as it is terribly metallic.

Sitting on the toilet thinking this through, I couldn't muster that much upsettedness over Irina's awful inquisition of Kahlo's famous and beautiful diary. I was too emotional (as I let out some well pent-up shit) over that Fuentes.

Fuentes, that's who I was *so* upset with. In the bathroom my emotions were flowing out faster than piss and shit. Oh my god. That unbelievable asshole. To compare a woman to a century of suffering? He does compare her. He lays her out right beside it all. She who was already laying out, so potable. He makes her live like that, in his introduction to her diary, *as* a century. As Auschwitz, Hiroshima, etc., what he calls "the rape of Nanking"—

"From the Armenian massacres to Auschwitz, from the rape of Nanking to the gulag, from the Japanese POW camps to the nuclear holocaust in Hiroshima, we have seen pain, we have felt horror, as never before in history."

Was she not in enough pain from her bus accident? From her true love for Diego, an asshole?

Carlos Fuentes, a woman is not a symbol!

I remembered then, in the bathroom, when I had taught the diary at the arts college. I had told my students, who were very upset, "Be careful, be careful about what you bottle up together in the same sentence. A period's the cork. If you're successful in your writing this stuff will live and pickle together for who knows how long. A sentence is a consigning." I told them also, "Rape is not a metaphor."

They were immeasurably upset about their debt. That's all they could speak of.

But someone in that classroom, the technology loose on its hinges, rats—yes, rats—and busted chairs like cubism, had said to me, "Iris"—they never called me anything else—"the Nanjing Massacre consisted of mass rape. It is not a metaphor." He was Chinese, he said.

"How can that be possible?" Is it possible, I thought—I went through scenarios—to rape many, many people? To build moving tableaus of just, rape. I didn't know. I panicked to feel.

I was teaching Kahlo's diary, I wanted them to know about aphoristic private sciences, her bed-science. They told me what happened to the Chinese in Nanjing. They all knew. They told me, "The banks are raping us, Iris," and I said I know they are but please don't use rape as a metaphor.

But they looked at me so betwixted. Were bankers raping them?

I was in the bathroom at The mARTin for a long time, reading over every review, sitting on the toilet still over my piss and shit. A lot of the exhibits there had been like that, about destruction, or what, these daring revisions? The heart-stepping cows were coming into focus in the context of The mARTin. Oh god. What was meant to happen with them?

"Why," I asked Caroline, back in the kitchen, "did you only read one letter, if you opened and went into my package? I mean, I was in the bathroom for a really long time."

"Oh, it was a little bit, you know, I got bored."

Caroline tried to look tired. It was impossible. She only looked relaxed, fluid. She finally handed me a fork (the kind with only three elegant, rustic tines), and some garlic salt. She opened up a bottle of fine violette.

It was not noon.

Food, hunger's Oxycontin, and all my stomach's pain and shaking and burgeoning individuation was over. Pécuchet said, "Good riddance. Pfft!" Bouvard was so asleep I thought he might have died.

"This would be my problem," Caroline was saying, "with someone like Lee Edelman, the queer theorist? He would try to *keep* the denial of reproductive futurity, he would hold *that* in opposition perhaps to something like heteronormativity, and heteronormativity, for him, would then express itself as a temporal regime that is also socially integrative and models its production on this configuration of sexuality that is also a production of the social order itself, and I would say 'Ugh,' because I think this is *also* among our normative suite of energies that we conduct, that the worlds we build together are often suicidal, implosive worlds, and maybe that's kind of mostly what we are doing." Attacking the eggs with my mouth and spirit I could hardly hear any of this. I'd never heard of Lee Eggelman I mean Edelman.

Why did Caroline find my dad's letter boring? What could have bored her? That my mom was sick? That my dad told my brother— right there in the letter—that his leaving us (and her in bed, neglected) was all my fault?

I took the letter out and read it to myself, to check for boredom. I could not be bored by it.

"Our fantasy," Caroline said, "is that there is a future. That is our fantasy. And we're not really capable of—we can't see through that. And we could point to any number of crises. The way we talk about ecology for example. Even the science of ecology itself is pointing towards all of our conspicuous consumption, our waste, but we don't ever ask ourselves, 'What are we actually doing?' We diagnose some things that are problematic, and that are destroying the biosphere, and that are making it unfit to live, but we're assuming we can change those things by intervening with policy or reducing carbon emissions rather than asking, 'But what are we actually doing? What do we seem to want?' We seem to want to make things unlivable for ourselves. We seem to want to spectacularly self-destruct by means of creating a social order that destroys itself."

"Dear Kenneth and Iris," I read, trembling and holding up the not-boring-to-me letter, "This Father's Day will be devastating for me if I cannot be with you. I had to leave, though, because I can no longer deal with the hurt of how Iris treats me. I feel very disrespected, and her anger towards me is too much for any dad to deal with. If I even attempt to speak with Iris, I get back a very contemptful and disrespectful response."

"Well, was it true? Did you respond like that?"

"I was fourteen."

"I bet you were one of those fourteen-year-olds going on thirty. I bet you were vicious!"

"We don't have much control these days. Mom's MS only gets worse. So it becomes a pressing issue, whether or not you're going to help. What can we control? The grass can be kept short, and the kitchen clean. I can only imagine this should be important and necessary to you as well. I know that it helps me. And what I would hope is that you would see: what helps me helps you and, these are pressing chores. Anyone might understand that the chores I assign to you are common jobs kids do across the country."

Caroline was laughing over her violette, drinking and snorting. She put her legs, athleisuresque, up. "Oh my god."

It's not boring if it makes you laugh. Her bun was lots larger than her head.

"It's silly. It's dumb." She poured me more violette, straight up. "I mean, that poor Kenneth!"

"Kenneth?"

"Did he ever return that box to you?"

"Yes. But at school they'd asked him to label it and he did. He wrote his name, in pen, on top of it on the lid."

"Surely in pencil?"

"No, in pen. And the box was a very soft wood, think of cigar boxes, so soft, so his name was ravine-like in the wood of my box."

"What did you do?"

"It was returned to me. I put a bandaid over his name."

"And you put your things back in there?"

"I think so."

"That was dumb."

"But," I continued, "maybe you don't understand. Maybe things Mom says to you are in conflict with my own expectations. Then it would not be your fault not having clarity about a chore. Please refer, then, to the chart, and remember that you both pledged to follow it closely. Because of the chart, there should not any longer be food left in the kitchen, clothes all over the landing, or grass mowed at unbecoming diagonals."

"It's very work-will-set-you-free, you know? And did they, your parents, punish Kenneth for dishonoring your trust in him, to take your box with him to school?"

"It was understood that Kenneth *had* to write his name on my box, if the teachers wanted everything labeled like that. Kenneth could not say no to his teacher. And yet, Kenneth often imagined persecution. Because of everything. Probably because my dad survived."

"Your dad was a survivor?"

"He was born on the *way* to Ellis Island, on the ship. His parents' other children had not survived. Maybe it was an avenging, to have him on the boat, or a triumphant procreation—or maybe it was ghosts or refractions going through motions?"

"Your family bowed to the authority of Kenneth's teachers but it was really Kenneth's story about authority, and his imagination of persecution, and all this inflexibility, as though he were at a camp. I wonder what he thought would happen to him if he did not write his name there, on your box? How could they submit to this story? He could have attached his name to the box with a length of masking tape?"

"But you feel bad for him when I read you the letter?"

"Of course I do. If this was his nature, when he was, say, ten or eleven, think of the Kenneth—fifteen, sixteen?—who received this letter from your dad. This letter isn't really written to you, that's obvious. And look at you, all very lovely in this jumpsuit, almost as beautiful as Irina, and he's had to live like this I imagine the rest of his life, used, really. You have no idea how beautiful she is. Wait."

"Being good kids," I read, "benefits the group. Once given a task, finish it fully and correctly. Good kids at school know all about finishing their work, and it appears your teachers find you to be this sort of kid. So bring that dedication back into our family."

"Do you see what I'm talking about? Poor Kenneth."

"I am incredibly proud of both of you. Kenneth, your school work, the fun you have with your friends, who you are as a cheerful boy. Iris, your performance in the play stunned me. You have dazzling looks and a great sense of humor."

She only laughed.

"Don't you see that this would have destroyed me, Caroline? I was so young."

"It seems to have been a bit of an attempt."

"It's sad but I can't come back to the house until I see both of you demonstrating the principles of basic respect. Of course it is unfair and possibly scary that now I can't be there for Mom. What I know is that our family needs to change."

"Why don't you just burn it? Here, on the stove?"

"I don't want to! He ends, 'I hope you will consider these thoughts seriously.'"

"Well, you have. Poor Kenneth. And your poor stones and stickers, they had it made in that box, in that cool rainbow steamroom you made for them, oh well."

It was past noon.

We'd moved to a blue fernet.


"You need to tell me, if I'm going to work for you, did you kill your husband? Is that what happened here?"

"I believe," said Caroline, "we need a theory of universal history, but to show that it's present at every moment and that all kinds of things are happening. But the trouble we most often have is trying to distinguish between something that's pathological or is an aberration and then another thing that's just there, that's running alongside—and I'm trying to suggest we do it, murder, destroy, alongside all these other things we're doing, so what are the forms of universal history that are operating and what do *they* seem to want? What are they good for? Can we consciously construct a genre of world history that isn't obliquely and also joyously self-destructive? But in all of this destruction there is also obscene creativity. There's so much deep jouissance involved. A kind of delirium is present all over the place. I don't know what the outside is. But it is clarifying to discover the drama of these global convulsions—the camps, Nanjing—in these little moments (your minor box) that we take to be so intimate."

"How did you do it? In which room?"

"I don't think we know what we want. We want everything. We want all of it. And principally we seem now to be capable of collapsing what is singular, and isolated, and what is universal. Those things now have collapsed, Vivitrix. And I don't know what this *we* is—a strange grand organism that is all kinds of things. That is both the planet and not the planet and infinitely more subtle. We can't actually distinguish between what we want or what we don't want. Or maybe we want things that are actually quite nightmarish. Or we want things that are proliferating all kinds of unthinkable possibilities. And I think it's because we're not at the center of ourselves anymore. If you think you're speaking in your own name about what ought to be the case, maybe you're already participating in this world that is very interested in destroying itself, and part of that is thinking you're only a part and that you can step right out of it. That's a kind of looping psychotic production of auto-spectacle that can do so much more than it is aware of. I think we're more powerful than we realize, yet our reflective capacities . . ."

"And why? Why did you kill him? What was your intimate reason?"

"We *can* still say things, Vivitrix. I even think the difference between *doing* and *saying*, even that has been surpassed for at least fifty years. It's no longer—I don't even think that's a good distinction. So the difference between words and things or actions and events, let us say in our social, civil, technical order, has been obsolete since at least the middle of the century. It also seems to me that we are doing so much more than we are aware of. The problem is not that there isn't enough power. The problem is that there's way too much power. There's so much power that we experience it as passivity and inertia and as incomprehension or as being overwhelmed. We are overwhelmed by our power."

"You were overwhelmed by your power?"

"I'm not talking about individual subjects. I'm talking about a networked organism that's doing all kinds of things. Like an infrastructure. What kind of infrastructure are we? What cloud of proliferating futurities are we? *What kind of cloud are we*, I'm not sure, and further, how is that cloud dreaming to itself? What forms of intelligence, what forms of reflexivity are the necessary initial degree?"

"Was Matthew involved?"

"No, Viv. It was not with him at all. Leave him out. And it's not that we need to cultivate new resources or new virtuosity. It's already out there. There's so much happening. Our grotesqueness is that we suffer from an excess of capacity."

"Does he know?"

"What is happening when there is gentleness, V-trix? I would venture when we look at places where gentleness is happening there is something like an extreme intelligence and an extreme agility of managing relations. I don't know. I don't know." She cried. She broke down. But it only looked beautiful, almost like vogueing, her elbows Rohmeresque in the kitchen. She could not help herself.

"I think he might want to know."

"He knows!" She looked up, uneasy, incredulous, possibly sly. In any case a delight. "It was all just, necessary. Irina knows. A lot of people know. Martin was a problem, that's all. He was deranged. He was, I don't know how to put it to you, Vivitrix, he was very, very boring."

# PART 3 / BILLY THE ID

Bouvard said, "A sunrise is a trick, Pécuchet."

"How's this?"

"It is posed to us as a great event, one of the truly great things to see. But to look at the sun is to go blind! It rises like this, so extravagant, like a yolk of pure glistening sailed into blue oil. It's very beautiful, Pécuchet, but when we go to look, as the gurus recommend, we get clusters of these spots all over the inner film of our seeing, do you see them?"

"Yes, I do! Bouvard, are we—is it—are we dying?"

"No, no, but these spots, this rash of dotty polka dots, out of order, in a cluster, fucking up the air and the grass and books, might be with us for a little while. Now, close your eyes."

"I'm doing it."

"You are?"

"Yes." Pécuchet was closing his eyes.

"Now see how they turn into something like a constellation or a map. The dots, which are all the sun, are all *the spawn* of the sun, make these tempting maps right there on the interstice—do you see that? Can you make out your map?"

"Yes. My god. It floats in a black sea. Its pattern is rigid and intact. I can't shake it." Pécuchet shook himself like a dog.

"Yes, it's no matter how you shake or squeeze your eyes. Mine is the same."

The retirees both squeezed their eyes and shook themselves.

"Now, what I'd like to know, Pécuchet, is if our maps are the same or are they different?"

"My god. We'll have to describe them to each other. You start."

"Mine is a column of orange dots with sear-like streaks, gashes of blue and green. The column deviates. Is yours like that?"

"No! Mine is totally different!"

"What is yours like?"

"Something else. I can't imagine how to say it."

"Pécuchet, *find* the words. We need to know each other's maps, to understand."

"How do I begin?"

"How weak you are! What color? What color is your sunspawn?"

"It changes. It changes! Though the map doesn't move. Is it a map? A pattern . . ."

"My god, don't tell me about variants! We can't track those. We should embrace what is invariant, constancy shall be a source."

"For what? What will constancy give us?"

"Is your pattern like a column with a splitting path at the top?"

"No. No . . ."

"Is the splitting path at the bottom?"

"Not even close." Pécuchet wept, to confess his difference from Bouvard.

"But we both see these spots. We are both so impacted by the light."

"We both are nearly blinded by the sun."

"The museum does not look empty now, to me, Pécuchet. Now that we are back inside of here. These marble walls fill, everywhere I look, with my own split column. It's very cheap. Very reproducible. But very individual."

"That's grand." Pécuchet opened his eyes. He saw his dots stamping repeats through The mARTin. I only meant to be inside for a moment, to use the bathroom. The sun was still very much rising and I wanted to see it all the way up to the top.

Matthew sat there on the toilet clapping. "Is this the playwright?"

Pervert. He'd intentionally not addressed the bolt. But, by grace, was clothed, perched on the toilet in the outfit of an international type of asshole—black jeans, a cuffed severe shirt, pointy leather shoes in a high brown like the end of my period.

Smart. The bathroom is an excellent place to catch a guest. A bathroom has its undeniable magnetism, toilets are made of such magnetic porcelain. This was a very good bathroom. There were undoubtedly many others in this huge place, but I'd been told that in the off months (all *eleven* of them), and besides whatever was winging ensuite off their private bedrooms, this was the only one open to the poor cowherd I'd really truly become.

Poor, I had slept the night out with the heart-stepping cows of Sachsenhausen, being offered no housing or health insurance or mental health insurance. Lots of booze, ultimately, though. Care is uneven.

Most of the night a hoof could be found on my heart as the cows took turns. I would never have been there, in the farmer's grasses in the first place, trying to escape. Sachsenhausen was a *work* camp, you had to work until you died. Sorted for use. I don't think I would have been sorted for that. It's so mean to sort, to type. It's really mean to murder, to write, I mean, obviously . . . I mean that I wouldn't have been there in the first place. I would have been sorted for the gas, looking so despicable and useless as I can. Too thin. These cows were doing an awful thing, but in the high grasses of The mARTin I couldn't help but feel *loved*, these cows not applying any pressure. It felt like they were taking care, even if it was so that a theoretical and long-dead farmer could take his own shot. My beating heart in the grass kept them up, they could not settle down if there were a heart. I said a prayer for that American boy who'd died and for the parent who should never have taken him abroad and treated the farm upending the work camp at Sachsenhausen as any kind of discontinuation of that place, as if the camp does not change its form to farm, easy, the cows with barracks for their bones, or their barn but a pentagram in a square wooden gown.

Everything is everything else, is a thing.

The camps, I shook my head, no DO NOT ever end, but I fared luckier than that kid, I would say. I did not have a particularly weak heart like that little kid. That was not my problem. The heart isn't joints.


Dung smelled, to me, like dark chocolate made out of wet rope.

"This drubbing!" said Bouvard.

"I am at the end. I am really at the end," sobbed Pécuchet.

"Let's distract ourselves grandiosely!"

"How? I am clobbered. I am defeated." He whimpered.

"What does this dung smell like to you, dear Pécuchet?"

"Am I meant to distinguish between smell and taste?"

"It is notoriously difficult to describe a smell. It's rarely even done, yet smell connects us to our past, to a sexual interest, it warns us off of a bad scene, and when someone dies it is their smell that lingers in a chrysalis in an ether, always up and away, always. We resist it, but smell needs language more than any of the other feelings."

"You mean senses. This dung smells like a homeopathic dogshit."

"Yes! Péc! That's good!"

"This dung smells like shit with burnt cookies."

"That's all right . . ."

"It smells like hot tree pudding."

"Pécuchet, you're grand. You're being grandiose!"

"I'm hungry."

The dung muffled their mouths but they went on like this all night, loud in the dung, and I thought, what herb, medicine, diet, death, or other practice will snuff them out of me forever?

A new cow came upon me. It was one after the other with these cows. I yelled down to the retirees, "Shut up! Please be quiet!"

This new cow was a bit rough in her mount but she lightened up. She held herself hollow. Good. They were all out, encircling me and taking these turns. My heart beat, so. My feet hurt. Pécuchet had said, "Vivitrix, do you see any of their calves?"


Matthew. Thronemugging on the toilet, holding a stack of papers. I had to go so badly. I squeezed at myself. And I needed tampons.

I had never seen him before but he looked refreshed. He seemed to look better than he'd ever looked. But this was a bathroom that made everyone look good. And it smelled good, like sage and bleach and—were there any tampons? He looked young, like a young springy forty-five-year-old, so maybe Caroline really wasn't ninety-five years old. Or maybe he was thirty, or sixty. It depends on if someone looks *really good* or *really bad* and he seemed like someone who looked quite good.

"Who's Iris?"

"Iris?"

He showed me his papers, a printout of a scan of the legal pad in my package, where I had written half of the play "Billy the Id" at seventeen. So Caroline had gone through everything. She had snooped and she had scanned. I needed to go to the bathroom. I needed a 3-D print-out of a tampon.

"Oh. I see. Iris is a character I wrote about in this play I wrote when I was seventeen."

"And who's this Billy?"

"He's, like, a representation—like an embodiment—of the id?"

"Really clever."

"Well, I was seventeen."

"Really clever for a cowherd."

I had been warned he would be "Heathcliffish," but what does this mean? I looked at his skin. It wasn't swarthy. You can't be Heathcliff, actually, if you aren't bearing the abuse that comes from racism and colorism, ignorance and nationalism, poverty and power. Was he Heathcliff merely because he was an undermining person, willing to pervert up families for revenge? Was he Heathcliff because he was handsome?

"Can we continue this conversation after I have used the bathroom?"

"Are you going to flush, Iris? Eh?"

He was referring to a main characteristic of my character Iris— she forgets to flush.

"My name is Vivitrix Marigold."

SCAR!

I sang him my whole song, in the bathroom. Because I felt like it. Because a bathroom has the best acoustics. Because I wanted him to call me, and know me as, Vivitrix Marigold. Because I felt like singing. Because this was a music video. Because I was bleeding out of my cunt, etc.

> I have a scar on my knee
> I am sitting there
> What is the thing I see
> It's not blood anywhere

> Because I am SCARRED!
> I'm scarred, scarred, scarred, scarred, scarred

> I am SCAR!

> If I had blood on my knee
> From getting hurt badlee
> That was, that was
> It was a long time AGO! And now I'm SCAR!

I had blood on my knee
I was just sitting there
I had fallen down and on the asphalt arms
Of the WORLD!

The blood was dripping down
The floor was getting so
red, red, red, red, RED!
But now I'm SCAR!

That was a long time ago, that was a long, long, long, long,
    long, long
time AGO!

SCAR! SCAR! SCAR! SCAR!

When I was sitting there
A strange man enterèd
He looked at me but did not see my knee
all dressed in coming blood
He said GET UP!
He said YOU MOVE!

I bled quietlee for a long, long time.

I bled until the blood was mar-i-GOLD!
I bled until my skin was blue, blue scales.
I bled until the scales came OFF!

That was a long
That was a long
That was a very very very very very very long time

Went.

Later he met me in the field. I had spent a short amount of time on my phone, in the bathroom, learning how to be a cowherd on YouTube and Wikihow, and had found myself a bucket in their kitchen. I was going to milk the cows manually, as I could not find or make milking machines. There was so much dung caking my feet, those fellows, I was going barefoot now, but fortunately the land was spongey with rain, the whole fields enough (for the moment) like a big quilt of orthotics.

I had washed myself (hands and feet) in the fountain out front, watching the sun catch on those metal letters of The mARTin. The bones in my feet felt stressed out. There was a lot of visible inflammation around them. I gripped and held both of them, in the guise of washing them, hugging myself, a group hug.

I was milking a cow real good.

I had been so goddamn desperate in the bathroom. Caroline was post all of that, there was nothing in the cabinet below the sink. No tampon. I cursed myself for never mastering a Diva cup. Never finding the right fold. I used the last of the toilet paper for my piss and shit. I was in so much blood trouble. I just had to do it. I just unframed the dumb thing. I just rolled it right up. This old paper from the '6os was just quite absorbent, it almost had a homemade quality. Old paper like that is made out of rags. Really. *Sleeping Nude and Man Writing*, you were but a sketch. But I painted you.


"So my mother told you about Dad, I hear."

I still was thinking about what to do with all this milk. The internet doesn't like it for soil, unlike menses, which could feed and replenish the worms and more. Nobody wants milk spilled in a creek or on the rocks in the grass.

"Can you tell me why there are no calves at all in this bunch?"

"You mean herd?"

"Yeah, herd."

"It's not a big deal. He was asking for it and it happened one day."

"How did he ask?"

"He was feeding her vicious insights about me. She'd been hearing them all my life. It was making her sick."

"What were his insights?"

"Oh, nothing. I was gay."

"You were?"

"No . . . I think he was looking for words for his hatred. That one came up. There were others."

"Why did he hate you?"

He looked perplexed. "Iris," he said, "there *is* hatred."

"Was he going to hurt you?"

"He was never going to hurt me."

"How did this happen?"

"It was very simple. We buried him there." He pointed at the upper field.

"She said you were not involved."

"I was not involved in what killed him."

"What did the killing?"

"I think you should ask her, if you really believe that matters. What are you, looking for ideas?"

"I wanted to know why there aren't any calves with this herd. An average dairy cow has two to four calves in her lifetime."

"Yes, Iris, but they don't all remain with her, do they? Only the female calves remain with their dairy mother. The male calves are separated and reared for breeding, beef, or veal."

"Right. So where are the female calves?"

"Maybe they didn't have any. Maybe the heart-stepping cows of Sachsenhausen really like having sons. What were you reared for, do you think, dairy or beef? They both have their advantages."

"Did Caroline use something very visceral?"

"You'll have to ask her yourself. When you're off duty. If you're that morbid and pitiless. I can see there's a lot of milking to do still." The bucket was mostly empty. The cows looked enormous and perturbed, some milling by me quite desperate.

"That's something I was hoping to ask about? What are my hours? Is there food here, or in town? May I sleep somewhere?"

He laughed.

"Sorry," he said. "'Town' is funny. You can come to dinner. Irina will be in, so we'll have our typical artist's welcome in the main gallery. Irina has requested a picnic . . . She's really fun. We have to get to work and start envisioning *things*."

Dinner, at sunset, was out on the main floor and nobody seemed remotely similar to how they ever were. I had told my students as much, "Don't bother writing a character since people change."

Caroline looked younger—fifty?—and wore a binding dress of gold, forcing her to sit in a very straight basic yoga pose. Forcing me to gaze at her long knees.

"But Bouvard, is gold a stone? Is that so? Is gold a gemstone—so would be a stone—or precious metal, so a metal?"

"Aren't there precious gems? Is there metalstone? This sort of thing!"

"No, I don't think gold is a stone but holds stones, as in a ring of gold. That is a golden *metal* ring. Right?"

"Which is deeper, metal or stone, or can there be flecks of metal inside and all over the tops of stones? Are there any golden gems to discover in the indexes?"

"And which, I wonder, dear Bouvard, is more valuable, more inestimable than anything else?"

"Gold is a material."

"Yes. Yes, let's set that down."

"It's a material that has worth."

"Yes. Like many a stoney gem, too."

"Right. But how do you flax it? Is gold so pliable? Or is this the gold of only a myth? Or marketing?"

"Gold could be melted. I don't believe you can melt, say, a topaz."

"Topaz! A common gem! A witch wouldn't even pick one up if there were some lying around on her porch."

"No. A witch would pick up a ruby though! I know she would do that."

"Pécuchet, what do you suggest, that we leave a ruby for a witch? I would think she would like to spend her afternoon playing with a diamond."

"Bouv, a witch would be beleaguered by a diamond! A witch prefers a ruby or an opal, and, above all, *the black pearl*."

"Pécuchet, you're very right, and have you seen a black pearl up close? It is green . . ."

"That is what she likes about it. It's witch's black, which is green.

But think of things. Think of the Black Forest looking more green, more brown, more marigold, and black bread almost made of a compressed red and brown foam, it's almost auburn if you hold bread up to the window. I don't think this woman, Caroline, is even wearing *any* metal at all, if indeed gold *is* a metal. Is it? She does not look so weighted down, not so *plated*, Bouvard. Is there such a thing as golden *silks*?"

"But silk flows, this dress is very *tight*. Is there a thing such as a hot tight silk?"

It was too much for them and I winced, to be barefoot on that kind of marble surface in the gallery, nothing to support my poor (and by the way idiot) feet. They were nervous. I put them nearer to each other.

Matthew was dressed in a suit, the food being cubes of huckleberry-enJelloed veal, roasted carrots with kale marmalade. Everything was labeled.

"Matthew, you're amazing."

I sat down but no one was introductory. Power tactic. I had milk and shit on me.

"Thank you, Irina. You're kind. We're so glad you're here."

Everyone ate. No one had said who I was. Caroline was staring ardently at the artist. Oh well.

I had told students, earlier, when I had such darling things, "Don't write about food in an inventive way."

"Why," they said. "Is that true?"

"It's a silly hole to go down. You don't want to come off like Bret Easton Ellis in *American Psycho* at this point."

"Iris," they said, "nobody cares about that guy. Who is that?" They told me they could not make it to the event because of suicidal family members, predation, assault, and work. My cares and outrages, concerning the craft, they said, were null.

"Do you like this, Iris?"

He was referring to the kale marmalade.

"It's so good."

"Irina brought it. It's semen."

"It is?"

She explained, "They grow baby kale in the bull testicles, they've been doing it in places in the south for a long time."

"You are all fucking with me. You Spanish do a lot to the bulls, but . . ."

"It's true! Do I call you Iris or Vivitrix?"

Caroline said, "Vivitrix," and Matthew said, "Iris!"

"It's true, Vivitrix. When the semen squirts out they immediately are mixing it with preservatives and also some gelatin, so that it doesn't, you know, *it stiffens*. They've been doing it for years in the rural area that I come from."

"I tremble over what finds its mount in the urns of tradition," said Bouvard.

"This is the delicacy she brought?" said Pécuchet, incredulous. "What a terrible Spanish lady! Bring a paste of quince, please! A *membrillo . . .*"

I had told those students, "Do not italicize foreign words," but I could not tell Pécuchet just then, not anything out loud. I had to be quiet. This was a crowd that liked to surprise and upset, that's all, I would need to explain to him. That's art, to these people. She wanted me chowing down on kale jam, kale cheese, the kale load of a big bull from her initial town. She thought I'd be so incensed, like, scandalized, but I only thought what I often thought—maybe it will help me.

"Sometimes," Matthew said, "there is nothing to say. You wish you had a script." He maliciously, just then, viciously and totally Heathcliffishly, handed out copies—yes, *copies*—of my play. When you look at a museum like that, in the country or anywhere, you know, if anything, it is full of, before all art, several scanners and some big industrial printers.

Irina snorted as she began to glance over the play. Here was a character flapping out of my largest wound. A confident woman. She wore nothing but pants and a shirt, like any actress at a cold reading. Bluejeans and a men's white shirt. She hardly had breasts. Her bra was vermilion, I could see it had glitter on the cups. I hated to look at her chest like that but my eyes went crazy diving for glitter in a muck of shirtmilk. It was inappropriate. "What is this?"

"A play I wrote when I was seventeen."

"It's not finished," Matthew said to me sharply.

"Children," said Caroline. "Don't fight. We have a guest." She smiled at Irina. Her enormous red-and-silver bun clashed with and initiated her dress.

"Are we all going to take roles?"

"Yes, give us roles, Matthew. Vivitrix, I assume you'll play Iris?"

"No, I want to be Iris," said Irina. She was reading ahead. She could see that Iris had most of the lines.

"Iris," said Matthew, "you need to be somebody else. Irina is our guest and a pretty established artist as well."

Pécuchet said, "I can't believe this. Are *we* going to get roles? There are five roles. There are five of us here. Don't tell me you all will double up leaving us wholly out of it?"

I don't think they counted me.

"And what? Do you think you'll play Billy?" said Bouvard to Pécuchet.

"You CAN'T!" I screamed.

Matthew looked fake-astonished. "Iris. We're definitely going to read this out loud right now."

I looked strange, his strange look said. He said, "Iris, you know what this is. It's going to be fun."

He took off his pants and read the opening monologue of that scoundrel, Billy the Id:

Ra! Ra! Let all parades converge and splurge! Let all dreams be gravy, all of you trudge through the mud like it's mythical potent gravy!

(waving bell wildly)

Mirrors are vaginas, John Updike said that, and I primp in front of them without shame—I see myself in them. And if they break—man, o, man—seven years of getting laid badly.

(rings bell)

Hear it? That's a thousand million moans of sexual delight, on this "pretty moon" of a night. Ladies are waving their breasts like triumphant flags, and man in general is thrusting his penis like a search light and projecting his crazy nipples into the crazier night.

(rings bell softly)

And that, my friends, is an enthusiastic cunt climbing up a set of limbs and kissing pubic hair.

(showers audience with bell)

Have you ever shuffled your lips up her neck? Did you ever know that tongues are the real mattresses at the bed & breakfast and hips are the best handles you'll ever handle?

(rings bell wildly, rambunctious on the stage)

Ra! Ra! Parades where the FUCK are you, already? Ra . . . Ra . . . Men come trampling in here, swinging arms and lips. Say: Ra! Ra!

(rings bell)

Hear it? It's the sound of men wearing capes and fancying themselves superman or God.

(rings bell)

And this? This one's for the smacking of bodies into other bodies.

(rings bell)

And this sound is the sound that sounds just before men's throats get braided together in battle. Then all is pretty fucking quiet!

(Picks up dictionary. Reading.)

Contraction of I would, I should, or I had! O wait. That's not Id, that's I'd. Hah! Id. Here we go: the part of the psyche residing in the unconscious which is the source of instinctive energy. Its impulses, which seek satisfaction in accordance with the pleasure principle, are modified by the ego and the superego before they are given overt expression.

Sex and aggression folks! I am Billy the Id!

See, some bored fuck up got bored one day so he went around and shot egos and "superegos" up everybody's ass. He died soon after, leaving everybody as one constipated mass.

So they proclaimed me Billy the Id and gave me this bell, which makes beautiful sounds, "The last quaking sounds of humanity."

Hear my bell! Hear my bell gratis!

Ra! Ra! Parades—where the fuck are you?

Parades! Parades!

(wanders off stage, ringing bell faintly).

"Iris—I mean Vivitrix," Bouvard said. My foot wheezed with pain. A knob hardened in each retiree. I needed help. "You can't let them do this. It's going to be too embarassing for you."

"But what about roles for us?" asked Pécuchet.

"You have to make them stop this."

"Caroline, I really want to know. Matthew says everyone knows here. Tell me, how did you kill your husband?"

"It was not a big deal, Viv. He would keep me up at night, that's all, hectoring me about Matthew, saying, yes, he was a, you know, that word, and also lazy, anything. I couldn't sleep, so I killed him with a hat."

"What kind of hat?"

"An adult bonnet."

"What did you do, suffocate him?"

"No, Viv, there were spikes inside of it. When he was nearly passed out I only secured this to his head. The spikes went in."

Pause.

"He was tied down of course."

"He died of multiple brain penetrations?"

"I guess so."

"What do you even mean by spikes?"

"Nails. I believe they were copper nails. We used them to kill trees when we got here. You put copper like that in a tree, or a person, it messes with the immunity of the tree, or the person. The tree attacks itself and dies inside, though it's still standing there. Even then you have to cut it down."

"But he was bleeding . . ."

"Sure, I mean blood killed him, I'm sure. I think he choked on it from his hat."

"And you used, what, this sun bonnet?"

"That would have been . . . No, I guess it was more like a sun-hat or something. Vivitrix, this is so not important. And everyone's bored. Irina already heard this and she's our guest."

"Is he buried in the hat?"

"Did we bury him, Matthew? I totally fucking forget."

"And now you're," I said, "going to kill these cows? Just checking. Is that going to happen?"

"The heart-stepping cows of Sachsenhausen?" Irina asked. "Oh, absolutely. Absolutely!"

"Why do that? Their milk is good," I said. "I mean, it works." I didn't know if their milk was any good or if it worked. I don't actually think milk "works." I don't know why I chose this angle anyway, to try to sell these cows as still usable, when my issue obviously was that I loathed these murderous artforms of The mARTin, did not believe in destruction as vision, not at that time, not murder. I wanted these cows to be scraped of origin and treated anew. Forgive them.

I wanted to live there.

"They're never going to stop coming up to people and holding them down, for as long as it takes, until a farmer comes to shoot them, Iris," said Matthew. I could see his penis.

"But why was he tied down?"

"Because I'd tied him down. He'd been drugged, I'd drugged him up, Vivitrix."

"And then you put the hat on him?"

"I just put it on him."

"To me, it seems inordinate."

"I think I might have hammered them into his brain at five different points in a pentagram, and then maybe put the hat over?"

"There was a hammer in the room?"

"It was in my hand. I *did* castrate him. *Then* I had it in my hand."

"You really can't castrate with a hammer."

"No . . . At first I had the tranq, in a syringe, then I used the rope, to tie his hands to bedposts, a paring knife, before the hammer came hard on those nails into his brain, the first going into the occiput, I think . . . Otherwise undressed . . . Let's see, I cut off his penis . . . Really, we didn't bury anything. What would there have been? I don't know where you get that, Matthew."

"When we moved here there were many more trees, which Martin wanted to get rid of, he really hated that."

Irina took a lap around the gallery, very slowly, mitigating her time during the repetition of this to-her-now-boring story. She sized up the white walls with her plans. But Matthew laid back on the marble, closed his eyes.

"Who hates trees?"

"Well, these were heritage trees they said we couldn't remove. What were they, Matthew?"

It was obvious she knew, she loved to involve him. He opened and rolled his eyes.

"The velvet trees, Mom."

"It couldn't have been real. They were telling us some natives, like some Native people, got a tree to copulate with a male deer, or probably the other way around if you think about it, and—You know they have that velvet on their antlers? It was a total bother, plus the story being bullshit. No animal is ever treesexual. It's a fantasy about, no a myopic inquiry into Native hortico-magics that distracts from expulsion, genocide, right? But really this kind of tree was a weed. That was the problem. And the 'velvet' was just *dark*. Dark dark dark like midnight gunking the property, morning was dark, every rooted thing just begowned in this soft, wet, and clinging version of a blackout curtain. The sun would wobble, would lose out around here. These velvet trees were like an elevator to a basement land. So we all wanted to do something."

My ears perked up. Weed, *weed*, a word like *just*, a warning word. When you hear *weed*, that scapegoated growth, you hear about power, a capacity. Track *weed*, that word we have for what grows without us. *Something is in it.*

"Are there any of the trees left?"

"Martin wanted them out, but he didn't want to be the one to do it."

"That was Dad . . ."

"I'm so sorry about this part, Matthew."

"I don't mind . . ."

"He had that little boy going around with a bucket—his little toy beach bucket, this *pail*—filled with copper nails, and this very real, this human hammer. How old were you?"

"Maybe eight, nine . . ."

"And he had to get these nails—you know, copper kills their nervous systems—all the way into them, in a ring around the bottom, and he couldn't come back for dinner until he did. And it was very dark, and Martin told him they were golden nails and that they'd form a track for the sunshine."

"Well, he was trying to figure out how to use me, Mom."

"He didn't understand your purpose. He thought, if I have to have this kid around, how can I benefit? That's what he kind of thought about parenthood, Matthew, 'Will I get yard work out of it.'"

I was cowherding the next day. The sunset was oozing.

There were usually at this hour a lot of chipmunks coming out of holes and running almost up the ramps of cows, but I was watching this big squirrel. So big. I wasn't used to it. It looked strange after looking at such buckets of chipmunks. A squirrel now, after all these chipmunks, wow, like a big baggy shadow of a chipmunk, like a chipmunk gone giant in her death, like her inflamous gray ghost.

"Do you want tea?" Irina asked. She said she liked tea that was rough, like a hammersmashed bush. She liked her water bitter, by tea or by tear, made quite complicated, she said. She had this beautiful jet-blue thermos.

"Ok, sure."

She drank her tea like a Turkish coffee, with no separation between the tea and the water.

"So you know," she said, kind of down to business, "since I don't know what you know—I would never *do* anything to Frida's diary."

"It was with your period blood though?"

"No . . . I had been working in Sachsenhausen for years, over two of my summers there, on a very matte lighting mechanism, so I could project from inside of the diary, so that I could make a little mystery, but it's not like I tricked everybody. But they (*The New York Times*) are really dumb."

"And why do you go there? Why do you, as Caroline says, 'summer in Sachsenhausen?' Is it some kind of Nazi light tech?" I imagined how some Nazis might want to use to their advantage a matte light. I thought of the torture potential of light not shining.

"No, it's a good residency, that's all. No one bothers you. There's very good funding. The application is so easy, too, and once you've gone you can keep going back, and you don't need to fill out a new application or ask for new recommendations from anyone. For a working artist, that's, like, *everything*. You can get an artist to live at a concentration camp easy, if there's a super streamlined application process."

"I see . . ." I had to keep up with my milking as she spoke. The herd was so taut.

"I have been hanging out with this herd for years over there—these are the very ones. I got them all to step on my heart a lot, too. In this year after the little kid died, it wasn't encouraged. But I think the herd missed it. So I'd go up at night, I'd be naked in the grass, and they'd be so eager to come over to me. And they had their calves with them, too, and were eager about that, passing it to them. They had these cute little calves stepping on me and getting it wrong. They had to practice, but it was ok because these little calves weren't so heavy they were going to kill me, so they could totally practice on my stupid heart. It was like a gang bang of heart-stepping out there, these little kids taking turns."

"How did the cows teach them to do it?"

"I *wanted* their weight, Vivitrix. I wanted to see if I *could* take it. I wanted the adult cows to step on me with their whole weight. I wanted to tell them that they could, if they wanted. Like, relax."

"Because you were committing suicide?"

"No. I thought I could take it, that's all. I really think I could. My heart feels incredible. I'm so strong, Vivitrix. I'm a runner and I meditate for two hours a day. I got kicked out of my house when I was a kid. I became Irina Olín, I developed my whole self, in a park in Madrid, in the anterooms of olive bushes, you know? That park was my high school, you know? I never even went to high school, or the doctor."

Were there such things as olive *bushes*? I wondered if she was lying? Art, you could say, the good lie. Or the true lie. It's not my thing, but people had said that to my students and they'd said that to me, when we were talking. But later they emailed me about all their problems that were so unreal.

"Did you need to go to the doctor badly?"

"I thought I'd really need to rely on that profession but it turns out there's prescription level stuff everywhere? Look around, you know? Look. There's all of this medicine. There's medicine, for example, in mouse enzymes, so I would go to work on some farms or at this camp for autistic children where they bond with some ponies, and mice live all over the barn. You can put almost anything into a syringe into yourself, almost at any point. You can shoot up your arms and butt and heart and neck and into the bottoms of your feet. I mean, what can't you reach on yourself? Are there parts of your own self you can't reach? I mean I can even shoot up my back, because I do stretch. Mouse enzymes helped me out, and honestly I was doing this intramuscularly, and everything in between, but, like, I stabbed myself in the heart once with a syringe I'd filled with my melted computer. It was an email, this email I wanted right into my heart."

"You don't want a melted computer in your heart, Irina. Oh my."

"You'd want this email in your heart any way you could get it in there."

"To preserve it?"

"No, I told you, Viv, my heart is really strong. I needed it in there, like putting this email into a cage with a tiger, a beast, a martial artist. I couldn't fight it with my eyes and brain any longer. I needed the heart to just take care of it how I knew it would."

"How did you melt your computer?"

"In a trashcan."

"Did the enzymes help you?"

"Just a little bit. I needed some further immunosuppression as well. But I was still very much young, fifteen, sixteen, so it was something to be careful about. You have to go with your parents or aunt or whoever to get these infusions and you do that every six months or so, that's usual, but I didn't have anything like that. My aunts died scrupulously. My father had written me this email in which he'd told me, 'You better not fuck us,' meaning him and his wife, because I needed some help with a security deposit. My joints hurt. I did not know he thought that about me, that I was a person who fucked him and his wife but that's what he said, 'Don't fuck us.' I think of that. I was in the park. The park was very wet. I had to look up where all this stuff exists, when I still had my computer. Nobody knows this stuff so you have to look it all up. I would ask people, even at pertinent meetings and at, like, scientific gatherings, 'Hey do you know what immunosuppression, like, *is*?' And they'd say, you know, where are your parents, but I was really dirty and reading Proust by the light of the moon in the park in Madrid and then later

128

in Seville, because I didn't really like being in Madrid, and Proust in Spanish is not that good, plus he was my great weakness. I didn't want to read Proust."

"What did you want to read?"

"Oh, I don't know, magazines."

"Ok, and did you get your infusion?"

"Well, I finally found out that what I really needed is a pretty high consistent dose of *any* chimeric monoclonal antibody, which is basically just a clone off a white blood cell, it's not a big deal, Vivitrix. If you have a mouse, you use the spleen . . . But you do have to fuse this with some myeloma cells. And then I did a hybridoma on that, growing the clone in a microtitre, but it's doable, especially if you have all this time. It's not like I was in school. I used this cute public microscope they had in the gardens of a science museum for kids. You put coins into it and kids would be in line all day to enlarge their hands or look at their cheek cells. It worked pretty well, actually. I went at night and used wooden coins I'd made and weighted with magnets. I kept jamming them in the microscope and worked all night until I could separate out the right cells, whichever ones were going to actually bind to the antigen. You can put those back into some mice if you want to grow some tumors that end up becoming basically fountains splooging out exactly what you need. You can milk a tumor like that, for your infusion, until the mice die, but I didn't do that, because I love all of life."

"So how did you produce the infusion?"

"I had to make cell culture, which sucks."

"And what did you do with all of this?"

"Diluted and injected, signed, sealed, delivered, Vivitrix. I couldn't really rig up an infusion station in the park, so I resolved to inject it a lot, *a lot*, to kind of keep up with the killing. You kill B cells, that's all. It's not a big deal. I think it was starting to work really quickly, because I was young. I'd be lying in the grass all day, thinking, and suddenly found my fingers could bend. I suddenly found that my tendons and bones were in harmony. They felt like the present, not like pain, or like the pain of a memory. I've kept up this pretty intense routine for almost a decade now. I always travel with a little refrigerator, and I really do prefer to fly."

"I can't believe you made all of that stuff by yourself."

"I'd lie naked for so long under these heart-stepping cows of Sachsenhausen. We know each other very well. I'd do it all night, letting them teach their calves on me, knowing at that point that maybe I would kill them, maybe feed them all to arts patrons here in New England. I knew I was going to buy them. I knew Caroline would help me do it even for half a million dollars. I'd lie there all night taking pictures of the different udders hanging over me—see?"

She showed me on her phone. The udders were granular, like Louise Bourgeois sculptures, in black and white. There was a cut through the udder, a bold black dripping line. She had her slim hand straight in the line, disappeared into the cove of the sculpture-like udder. A black-and-white photograph like that turns anything into a photograph of a sculpture. It wasn't fair, I thought. It seemed to me like a cheap trick, to use black-and-white photography in this kind of Germany, the camp kind, but it's good, too, I thought, to be lazy like that, as an artist. Especially if you're a woman. Fuck work. What was she doing, though, marinating her hand in an udder? What was in there?

"I love these cows, Vivitrix. I'm not going to do anything to them but love them."

"Do you want any of this milk?" I asked. My bucket was entirely full. I didn't want to walk down to the fountain again. My feet were killing me. What was I going to do? I was still so young.

"I don't drink milk." Irina looked horrified. "Milk is really inflammatory!"

She drank her tea. I drank some and it was so bitter and great. It was making me strong.

"That kid had such a weak American heart," she said. "It's not at all their fault. At all!"

"Do you know what happened? Were you there?"

"Yeah, he came a summer I was around . . . I tell you, Viv, he wasn't anywhere *near* any of these cows of mine."

She had her hand on one. A calf was behind her! They'd totally been there all along. Shyness is real.

# PART 4 / LAPIDARY CIRCLE

I was upset.

I was sitting at a table outside of Good Karma, the one right on Pine, reading a review in *The New York Times*, and Ray was late. It was not quite a critic's pick.

I was wearing a gold jumpsuit, a flax made, it seemed, out of the goldleafing on Gallimard's pleiad of Duras, and such hot pink shoes. Bouvard snoozed in the shade in a kind of dim library near a lamp that took its dulcet style from a dwarf willow tree. Pécuchet was sleeping too, on a bench. Wrapped up in his coat, which was padded with little notebooks in all of his pockets. They'd been back in Paris for a while now.

Why was Ray so very late? I was anxious to see him. I stared around terribly bookless, very friendless, very bereft and unfortunate. I'd heard he'd quit his job, so where was he? Was he writing? I swallowed—bored, very Plumless, very Dunnless and Naoless, and so pitifully Devotaless and Shimodaless, wasting away quite Ruoccoless—my new meds. I'd switched to a biologic drug with

135

my doctor's assistance, releasing the zest and the yeasts of the mice in me, after Irina. Between this and no dairy, and no calls to Kenneth, and Joe dead or to me, I felt really beautiful and smooth inside, really good. I'd told my students looong ago, "Don't make adult women reconcile or admit anything in your writing."

They'd said, "Iris, we can't afford to be here anymore."

One wrote me an email. He said his roommate was on suicide watch, he wrote "and I am that which watches."

"Is it true," Bouvard had asked Pécuchet, that very morning while these retirees, for the time being, were totally dying, "that the facts about the anti-Semitic persecutions during the Black Plague are quite well known?"

"Are you asking if I, personally, have known about them?" replied a drowsy Pécuchet, drooling onto his notebook, which was a bit too small for his fat handwriting.

"I doubt very much, Pécuchet, that *you* are an arbiter of what is well known to a general population, but yes, had you ever heard of it?"

Pécuchet yawned, doubly. About to drift off. "Where did you hear of such a thing anyway, Bouvard? Did you read about this somewhere? Should we not admit that all historical knowledge is uncertain and that nothing can be taken from *a text* as such, not even the reality of a persecution?"

Bouvard was also having trouble staying awake, but he was stirred by the debate a bit, "Pécuchet. Please. One must either do violence to this so-called 'text,' this historical record as it were—and written by whom?—or let that text forever do violence to its innocent victims!"

"All right, Bouvard. Ok. All right. Calm down my friend. So what are you saying? You're saying the Jews were scapegoated for all of the Black Plague? Is that it?" Pécuchet was wrapping himself in synthetic fleece on his bench but he wished for a big bed. His limbs sprawled on a wave of breathing.

"I'm saying, Pécuchet, that they were indeed, the Jews, the first victims of the plague, insofar as they were killed because they were blamed for it."

"Scapegoats!" Pécuchet burbled up.

"Last comes the ass, Péc, that least bloodthirsty of the bunch. Therefore, the weakest, and the least protected, you know . . ."

"You're right, Bouvard, of course you are right. One must not, it turns out, take too heavy an account, or have too sincere a relation, I suppose, with the text *of* a persecutor, no, no, that won't do, you're right, but I'm so tired now. I can hardly keep my lids up. You too? Come on now, let's get into the same bed. You know that when you are on one side of the bed it balances the mattress for me, on the other. But you know, I really don't think we can do away with these texts. The historical record? You would *think* the text is false, since it claims the victims as guilty, right Bouvard? But it's true, isn't it, doesn't the text provide *some* kind of truth actually, insofar as there really were *victims*?"

137

"I guess?"

"Let's sleep on it, dear Bouvard. Come on into this big bed with me." And the men did come together, balancing out an old mattress each for the other.

I'd read to Matthew my father's second letter:

Dear Iris,

I could hear how you were speaking to Mom. Again, it's that distant and clipped way you have with us.

Iris, we love you. I think I love you more than anyone else. You're an astonishing person and a talented would-be playwright—who breaks my heart with her anger. How can you bear this much anger? Maybe it is all of us, and we're all very upset, very angry. Something has to give.

Marriage is hard, and Mom's illness touches us in all aspects of life. She's brave on the outside but imagine how this all feels for her. And then for me, I've lost my activities partner and now everything we do takes planning and happens very slowly. I'm lonely.

About what happened in Gail's office. I'm sorry, but I was angry. And I stand by the things that I said, namely that this cannot continue. You cannot keep rejecting me—I need to see a sign.

What is responsibility? Showing us all, including Kenneth, that you care. You're never going to have a different family. And we're not so bad.

Iris, as I told you in Gail's office, I am not willing to continue in this way. The stress is hurting me too much. If you cannot find a way to reach out to us more, then I am sorry to say, one of us has to leave. I've been going over the edge of possible sadness one can experience. I think about how you used to be, as a goofy little girl, but now it's all about being pissed off, and staying distant. Not acceptable.

About your friends. Of course I like them. They're an impressive group. But are they helpful to us when they come over? Do they recognize that you cannot always see them, that we need you here with us? They can seem pretty oblivious to this, would you agree?

Parents all over this country are proud of their children's successes. Mom and I are even moreso as you and Kenneth are seen as healthy and full of possibility. I really don't mind your going off to become a playwright. I'll be so proud of how you pursue this dream so long as it contributes to society. We want to give you freedom and resources. But where is that responsibility I am looking for?

Stop this cycle and take initiative to save our family.

You've moved your bedroom to the attic but nothing's free. If you want to stay there, you should

- Do all household laundry
- Take out trash and recycling (sort!)
- Mow the lawn (front, back, side, including problem areas where the bees are)
- Keep the landing clear as water

If these bullets are not attended to promptly each week, you'll have to leave the attic. People slip up so let me know how I can help you stay in motion on these points.

About the car. We plan on paying over $1000/yr for insurance assuming you can get your license. But you don't qualify for good student pricing and this will cost everyone. Perhaps you will be able to work on that, and if not, you'll have to pay that portion.

In the best case scenario, you will show me that you love me, and care about my feelings here. You are a big part of my life, Iris. Even if I leave, or if I ask you to leave, we're a family. If you stay with us this year, before going off to college, let's all try to help each other out more.

Dad

"Hatred," Matthew said, "is inattentive, Iris. Even panoptic surveillance, methods used in a work camp like Sachsenhausen, intends to relieve the hater from having to keep up his watch. But even then, to watch? What is that all about? It's not like looking at something. My dad, for example, Iris, didn't know how many of these trees were even around the property. That wasn't his point, was it? Did the Nazis need so many sewed shoes? He wanted me working. He wanted to watch me work."

"I think you're playing a very dicey game, Matthew. I'm sorry, this is so not Sachsenhausen."

It was really nice at The mARTin.

"Whatever. I'm sure you've written your own letters, Iris, little lists of ways someone has just got to be, ultimatums for all your loving. I'm sure you've written just the same. The persecutory stink is no doubt all over. The persecutory strain, o, it roams."

"Of course I have! I've written that kind of list in a letter to someone I loved. He wasn't a child though . . ."

Matthew laughed very Heathcliff, "Hatred isn't organized, Iris!"

Very bitter.

I told him, "You know that Caroline refers to you as her Heathcliff?"

"She means that as a compliment, Iris."

"Heathcliff? He destroys everyone around him. He's so bitter."

He took this so personally. I had no idea.

"You don't know anything about him, Iris. Nothing."

"Matthew. I have read *Wuthering Heights*. You can't hide what's in *Wuthering Heights* from me."

I was concerned that because I was their cowherd they did not realize that I was a reader, a writer, and a professor of literature making at least three dollars an hour. I had taught *Wuthering Heights*. I had told my students, "If you love someone like Heathcliff you're pretty codependent."

"The narrator of that book, Iris, is the governess, right? She is such an asshole. Remember? I wouldn't trust anything you read about Heathcliff there. I'd look for him outside of that book. I'd go looking on the outside."

"She's not really the narrator, Matthew. It's actually a frame narrative."

He looked like he could have hit me. My students all knew a lot about codependence, and abuse, already. One sent me this pdf, *Why*

*Does He Do That?: Inside the Minds of Angry and Controlling Men* by Lundy Bancroft. She wrote, "I'm submitting this pdf as my radical revision of *Wuthering Heights*," which at the time I thought was a pretty good trick. She'd evaded writing, which is revising, I thought, because she had to go to work.

But Matthew only took out his pocket copy of the book, from his pocket, and read to me a very well-marked passage: "They entirely refused to have *it* in bed with them, or even in their room; and I had no more sense, so I put *it* on the landing of the stairs, hoping *it* might be gone on the morrow."

"In truth, I imagined the country to be different," said Pécuchet to his friend, Bouvard.

"It's true, Pécuchet, that you don't typically think of a museum."

That one, Pécuchet, the neurotic, had a sneezing attack, my bones searing and separating, feeling that pinstabbing coming on. That innerclobber. *I can't really walk.* That. At this point they were used to being incredibly dirty as I was never once offered a room. I don't think it occurred to anyone. And so they slept, my poor feet, if they could, on top of one another.

They began to beg me, "Iris, let's go back."

They wanted to find themselves back on Naudain St., they begged me. They said this was a failure—I needed my doctor, my doctor. It seemed so simple, like a tale, Don't ever trust a bitter pill. But they wanted for me only a bitterer one.

///

"I can't believe you're back."

"Wow, you look really great." Ray looked great.

"*You* do."

"You look really cool in your black shirt. How's it all going?"

Ray popped into Good Karma and got this cortado full of cinnamon, and then he sat with me at my little metal outdoors table glinting with the dusts early fall sunlight likes to embolden into bee crumble. Everything, surfaces, in such light fluffs up with this hyper-articulate crust I've really noticed . . .

"Well, uh, it's hard to say." Ray thought about it. "So much has happened and gone wrong, with the drain, and I've been out of my mind and don't know if I'm healing. I'm just going to assume it's going to get to a point that I'm going to be fine with. But it might take a while and I think I'm more upset about that because I'm impatient."

While I was in the country, he'd been filling up his post-surgical drains more than expected. Healing got out of hand. And when he had the drains taken out, it was always too soon, a couple of times. They kept putting a new drain in and he went to the surgeon in the spirit of minor emergency several times a week for weeks. Back and forth and alone.

"Joe left, I assume?"

"I asked him to leave. Iris, he's horrible. But Jess came up. She helped me. And she regrouted your bathroom."

"Jess?"

"She really helped me. I wish she hadn't left. I loved her company." Ray had been alone again, for months, while I was in the country.

"That's nice . . ."

"I could show you if you want? I have scar strips on."

Ray opened up, a bit, his black buttondown. This was the Good Karma on 9th and Pine, my cortado overbitten with its turmeric. Butterflies kept favoring our table, what madness. They looked like really vain angels.

"It looks so good."

"It still hurts, too, a little bit. That's also kind of a bummer. I'm sleeping on my back most of the time because this side hurts, oh well. It hurts because of all the drain traffic, but this side doesn't hurt very much. I'm sure if I were to press on it, it would, but."

"Don't press on it. Do you love it?"

Ray thought about it or sat there for a while, his shirt nicely open, a bit. He was taking testosterone. His voice was better. His novel was almost finished. I don't think he wanted to ever close it. The shirt, I mean.

"Yeah. But I've been just fixated and nervous about it because of the issue. But recently I've been trying to recognize that the drain is out for good this time and I get this rush of really loving it and kind of just in disbelief and I—I look completely different.

I'm excited. I should try some clothes on sometime and have fun or something."

He told me about his job.

"I told my boss if it comes down to it, I'm not going to be complicit in killing people for fifty grand."

"Wow, Ray."

"And then he called me paranoid. He thinks I'm mentally ill. And I was like, Gary, that's what happens when you put a person in a house with a surgical wound alone. This is a rational response. My anger and paranoia is rational. But then, I followed up in an email and I was like, I'm not gonna be complicit in spreading this disease so just take the whole fucking job if that's what you guys need to do."

"What if something really did happen?" Ray continued on Pine. "What if some people got sick? What if people died? I don't know how you deal with that. How would you deal with that? If something happened at your job—how do you account for that? How do you heal from that? I think we're all complicit in allowing this to happen. We know what's going to happen. How do you recover from that? Even just morally I'm saying . . . I feel like it's a line I don't want to cross for a fifty grand paycheck, you know? I don't need to cross that line. I don't have that much at stake here. It's like the line of no return. Like going to war, you know? Once you kind of very nonchalantly band together with a group of people and create the conditions for others' deaths, it's just, there's no turning back."

"I kind of need to move back in, Ray. Can I?"

"I couldn't live there anymore?"

"No, you can stay."

"Oh, then sure."

"Thanks."

"Yeah, you can move back into your house."

"No, no, it's yours. But also, I should tell you, Gracie II is dead."

"I don't know if I'm the kind of person who could get upset about that. I just can't believe you would trade a house . . . How did you get back?"

"My friend Maurice got me."

"Yeah, you can totally live in it. Yeah, if I ever sell it I can give you some of the cash."


The sun was beginning to set, a bit earlier than I'd been growing used to. It was 6 p.m. and you could see it heaving a little in the sky like it was about to throw up. Oh well. It was warm, but ribbons of crispness did exist.

"And did you see this awful article?"

"Yeah, what was that all about? Did you get involved in some art up there or something?"

"I was really just a cowherd . . ."

"Just! That's amazing."

Ray looked over the review. It was a full page in the middle of the Arts section.

"So the cows are all going to die by the end of this month?"

"That's the idea."

"And there are like these amazing beef buffets for the dinner guests?"

"Matthew's a chef . . ."

"He looks so handsome." A picture of him, out back, barbecuing . . .

"So in the gallery they're gonna hang all the hides?"

"Yeah, as they're killed, but they've all been branded with this letter from my dad, walking around the fields like that."

"What's on there?" Ray squinted. You could see in the photo the feast of beef, on long tables, piles intermittent with kale semen and champagne, and only that first hide nailed into the wall. September 1. The gallery was going to fill with thirty hide-copies of this letter, thirty cows completed, and, ultimately, these big chandeliers Irina was going to make out of skulls. A total punishment.

"They've been branded with this letter my dad wrote to me, when I was sixteen? He'd typed it up—two pages—and handed it to me in my bedroom. And then he sent it to me again, at the beginning of this past summer. That's why I was so upset at Good Karma before. I really had to get out of here. That's why I did something stupid, like

147

trade my house for your car. I'm sorry I didn't stay to help you post-surgery. That's what I should have done, obviously."

"That's all right. Jess was really who I wanted with me."

Ray squinted to try to read the letter off the photo, where it lay looking burnt into the one hide hanging there on the wall, tautly pinned by a pentagram of some copper nails or something. You could just applaud.

"I can't read this letter like this." Ray pulled up the review on his phone. I hadn't thought of it. He blew it up on his screen. He could read the whole letter.

"Oh gosh. Who the fuck is Gail?"

"Gail was my dad's therapist. I think he wrote me this pretty soon after this incident in her office. He'd gotten so furious in there—that office was like a tank for his fury—he'd lunged at me, and I'd run out. A friend picked me up. It was a really absurd night. I'd taken this job passing out fliers for a new fan website at a Britney Spears concert in New Jersey, so my friend picked me up from outside Gail's office—my dad and her were still in there, consorting or something, I swear they were in some kind of thing—and she drove me to Jersey and we gave out so many fliers to teenyboppers coming flushed from the stadium, two total dykes as far as they were concerned, one of us trembling."

Ray wasn't really listening to me. He was intently reading the entire letter.

"It almost seems to me," he said, "like he needed something from you that I'm not sure you could've given him, but it almost seems like he was convinced that you didn't love him. He was asking for something impossible, I think. The chores—this bullet-pointed list—are weird, they almost seem beside the point. Cause all that stuff about this is just heartbreaking for me, you don't love me, you used to be my cuddly little girl or whatever, it seems like he needs you to prove to him that you love him in this way that I don't think anybody could. You know?"

"Yeah. Sure."

"I wonder, why does he feel so rejected?"

"He'd spent my childhood being disinterested in me, in my adolescence he was cruel, and I wasn't speaking to him any longer. Plus I think he was having a bunch of affairs, around then, with women in his 'well-spouse' support group."

"This letter is so strange. It's so strange. And the housework stuff is just really weird to me. He's obsessed. And the way he wraps that up, like this is some huge failure on your part to not keep up with chores. This is way more than that for him. But every kid doesn't keep up with chores, I mean it's just weird, you know? And the way he's trying to reason with a teenager, like who cares if he doesn't like your friends? The source of the conflict is so strange. Because it's like this adult man who's having these kinds of strange teenage conflicts. It's schoolyardish or something, I don't know."

"Did you see what they say about it though?"

"In the review?"

"Yeah."

"This guy doesn't get what's so fucked up about it, I guess. 'Olín has branded a letter from a father to a teenaged daughter onto all of the cows she'll butcher this month. It's unclear if this was a letter Olín's father might have written to her or if it's just fiction. The letter disappoints, though.'—what??—'It's largest crime? Being boring. Here is a middle-class dad's typical angst over his daughter's lack of responsibility and the predictable insolence of herself and her friends towards him. He also points out to her that her grades at school don't qualify her for a discount on her car insurance. The recipient, whether it is Olín or not, seems only selfish, as teenagers typically are, and the father is having none of it. Alas, it's nothing to kill the cow over. The show, while grandiose in spectacle, and with Olín's usual flare for trickster bathos, like with what she did to Kahlo's diary, fizzles at the level of this completely unremarkable and totally mundane letter. Get over it, you know?'"

"I'm so embarrassed."

"Iris, that's rough."

"I don't think he even read it, this prick."

"Did your dad's therapist, like, support him?"

"Gail—I don't know what the deal was. But she watched as he lunged at me and didn't do anything. Which to me was one of my traumas in life, that I feel that my dad lunged at me constantly and nobody ever did anything about it. Nobody ever said to him, 'You stop that.' Everybody was expecting me to handle it or be ok with what he was doing or they really saw me as the powerful one, as the one making him do it. I mean, it was dangerous. It was so scary. That he thought of me as his equal."

"And he says here, 'Iris, as I told you in Gail's office, I am not willing to continue in this way. The stress is hurting me too much. If you cannot find a way to reach out to us more, then I am sorry to say, one of us has to leave.' It seems borderline illegal, right? Aren't you obligated to house your child?"

"He saw me as so powerful, I don't think he could see me as a child he had to house."

"Also, what's so disappointing about it is the generalities in the letter, you know, it almost seems like, if you were to please him, the best he could say is, like, you know, 'You're a great girl who contributes to society,' the most broad statements about you."

"I don't know how to think about these letters, because they hurt me so badly when I received them. When I was sixteen I wanted to kill myself when I got this letter. There was no way out. And when I was thirty-six and I received it, I had to get out of here. I couldn't even look at my house. You know that's my mom's house? She left it to me, I think she must have been so sorry about everything. *The New York Times* simply cannot read this letter! I should never have let Irina do this with it!" I wailed. "They don't see what it was all about. They can't feel what this was for me. It was beyond the letter. It was everyone else, he owned them. They mimicked him. He was setting up these conditions for who I was and how I should be looked at, and punished, and I knew nobody was going to be there for me. The farmer comes up and shoots you, fine, you're shot in the head, ok, the farmer's some kind of good German, but the cows? The cows? They don't even know what they're doing. But they do it."

"That's why the letter is so creepy, Iris. It's sprinkling in demands that seem conventional for teenagehood. Like, please do the laundry and mow the lawn. This thing about cleaning up the landing? So I don't know how someone would read this. I mean, I find it fascinating."

"I was worried that sharing it invites people to think, 'What's the problem?' And of course it wasn't that bad in some sort of comparative scheme or, I don't know, there's a lot of really bad traumas in families, but this was mine and it killed me. I guess I'm a little sensitive about how boring it turned out to be, it's just some dad ragging on a teenager or something."

"I don't think it's boring. I think it's sick. I get the fear that somebody would say 'So what' or something. But I would do something with it. This letter basically shows people what scapegoating looks like, at least in a letter form. He's basically saying,

'The family's success or failure is in your hands.' And then he gives you this weird bullet list of chores combined with this impossible demand to love him—you know, it's such a mindfuck, I would publish it if I had a letter like that. Why did the artist put it on these cows?"

"Irina was interested in thinking about generations of survivors of the Holocaust and she found out my dad was a survivor or sort of a second-generation survivor."

"I like it. A lot. I think that is a good context for the letter. They are both these two overwhelming things. The history of genocide and your terrible father. Both of these things can feel just as future-negating and they can both exist at once and they can both be totally dismissed as well. You don't have to think about genocide or give it much thought nor do you have to really understand why somebody's father was such a traumatic presence in their life. It's so easy to dismiss both of these things. It's really grotesque."

"Thanks, Ray. I hadn't thought about how anybody could magnify the screen, too, or whatever. It overwhelms."

"But why did you come back? Sounds like the show is all month. Don't the cows still need to be, like, herded up there? Don't they need help with this trick, to pull it off?"

Ray smiled.

"Oh, you know?"

"It's pretty obvious, Iris, this is all felt and velvet and, what is that, a little horse hair or something? Even in these photos you can tell it's portobellos. What are they, hiding the cows in some upper field? It seems cool. These people seem kind of neat. That guy Matthew looks really handsome. Why did you come back here?"

"The arts college offered me *two* new classes for the fall, I guess they're pretty desperate. They're going to give me 3,200 dollars!"

A scapegoat is, if anything, super grateful. Everything feels so nice and great. You want to do all kinds of things. You're a very eager girl.

"Iris, that's pretty nice."

"Oh. By the way. Call me Vivitrix."

"What?"

"Vivitrix Marigold. I changed my name."

"Um. That's weird."

"What do you mean?"

"After Gracie died, when my mom killed my dog? When I ran away? I went to a boardwalk. I was on the boardwalk and got pulled into this songmaking station where you can record your own single. It presses out a professional-looking tape? I sang this song, I can't remember, it was ok, but I know I called myself Vivitrix Marigold. So that's weird."

"Oh. Do you want the name back?"

"No, I'm probably Ray. For now."

"Should we get going?"

The sun was setting. It was making the bricks quite articulate. That's Philly for you. We got up. Ray fortunately kept his shirt somewhat unbuttoned. I resynched my golden jumpsuit. And we felt very moved as we went through it.

**PART 5 / 4.**

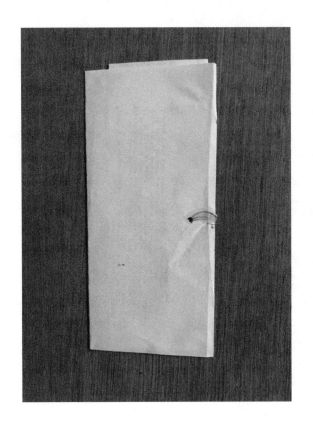

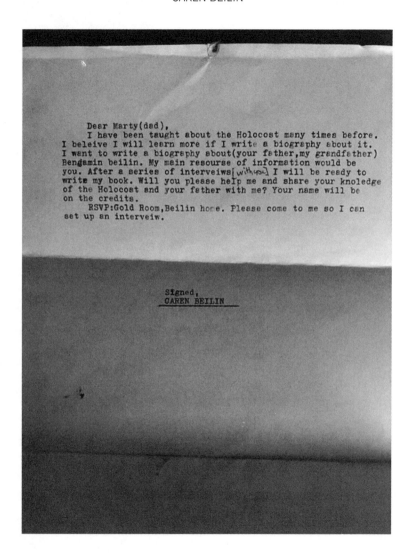

Dear Marty(dad),
    I have been taught about the Holocost many times before.
I beleive I will learn more if I write a biography about it.
I want to write a biography about(your father,my grandfather)
Benjamin beilin. My main resourse of information would be
you. After a series of interveiws[without] I will be ready to
write my book. Will you please help me and share your knoledge
of the Holocost and your father with me? Your name will be
on the credits.
    RSVP:Gold Room,Beilin home. Please come to me so I can
set up an interveiw.



                    Signed,
                    CAREN BEILIN

# A POSTSCRIPT ON METHODS

I don't want to write alone and two people, in particular, were down with allowing their voices, awesome wit, and life experiences to be a part of my revenge.

Caroline's thoughts on the family being lifted from a recorded conversation with Jean-Paul Cauvin, one warm and unhinged morning at the bun café . . .

My conversations with Ray Levy were recorded in May, 2020, and so between Virginia and Massachusetts via Zoom. I have used Ray's exact language from these transcripts in most cases except for minor areas where I needed to drive the fictional plot, and I've kept their real name intact at their request.

# NOTES

Pgs. 10–11: This Maurice Blanchot quote comes from his book *The Writing of the Disaster* (as translated by Ann Smock).

Pg. 18: For a nonfiction account of how my mom left her marriage and the suburbs, after living with MS for decades, how she moved to the city and began life anew, see my previous book, *Spain.*

Pg. 42: For a nonfiction account of how the copper IUD triggered my first rheumatoid arthritis flare, and how many IUD-users experience depression, anxiety, joint pain, the early onset of autoimmunity, hair loss, heart palpitations, and other life-altering problems, see my previous book *Blackfishing the IUD*.

Pgs. 136–138: Bouv and Péc's discussion about reading the texts of persecutors is lifted, in part, from Rene Girard's *The Scapegoat* (as translated by Yvonne Freccero).

## ACKNOWLEDGMENTS

To all my friends, with all my love.

To Ray.

To Gustave Flaubert (always) for giving us Bouvard and Pécuchet, and for my love, JP, for respectfully speaking to each of my feet.

To my dad, who sent the most ingenious novel-writing kit in the mail, which I appreciate. And for the more recent letter on Yom Kippur, appreciated as well.

To my mom and sister who miraculously and daringly support my prosess. That's love.

To my outrageous, out-of-the-box, keen, and curiously brilliant students at the Massachusetts College of Liberal Arts, and everywhere else, and to my wonderful colleagues.

To the Clark Art Institute and particularly its grounds and forest tenders. This open area, and the jut of your inquiry there, provided fertile space for my own wounded imagination. And to the cows, their tenders, and in recognition of Analia Sabin's art-fence for them, "Teaching a Cow How to Draw," which gave me, all summer, good shapes.

To goats, and Canaries.

To Julia Cameron—wow.

And to those people who were particularly there for this one, offering their own family stories, solace and/or encouragement, and even their presence in the text (for comfort, for courage, and because they're such good company): Ray Levy, Jean-Paul Cauvin, Hilary Plum, Raphael Dagold, Kristen Jean Gleason, Maurice Baynard, Jess Alexander, Zach Savich, Zack Finch, Joanna Ruocco, Caryl Pagel, Joanna Howard, Aaron Shulman, Alyssa Perry, Lauren Hamlin, Moire Conroy, Steven Dunn (and his Etch-a-Sketch), Vi Khi Nao, Catherine Lacey, Semyon Khokhlov, Emily Marker, Kyle Williams, Nabil Kashyap, Jeremy Davies, Jacob Kahn, Karin Dahl, Lois Harris, Emily Watlington, J'Lyn Chapman, Lisa Schumaier, and Brandon Shimoda.

And to Dorothy. Thank you Danielle Dutton and Martin Riker, for your amazing embrace. For this amazing home for sentences you've built, and all Dorothy authors, too, whom I've been hoping to get to go swimming with.

# ABOUT THE AUTHOR

Caren Beilin is the author most recently of a nonfiction book, *Blackfishing the IUD* (Wolfman Books, 2019), and a memoir, *Spain* (Rescue Press, 2018). She teaches creative writing at the Massachusetts College of Liberal Arts and lives close by, in Vermont.

Dorothy, a publishing project

DOROTHYPROJECT.COM